Praise for
The Last Boy at St. Edith's

★"Sweet, funny, exciting—
a spectacular debut."
—*Kirkus Reviews* (starred review)

"Humor mixes with
more serious issues in
this clever debut."
—*Booklist*

"Malone's debut is a sweet,
candid novel about fitting in,
messing up, and making amends."
—*Publishers Weekly*

Also by Lee Gjertsen Malone

The Last Boy at St. Edith's

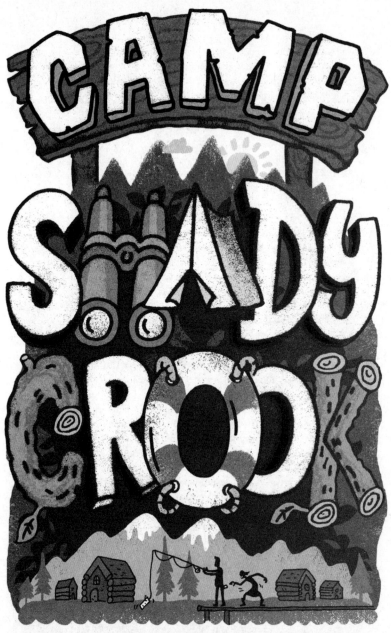

CAMP SHADY CROOK

LEE GJERTSEN MALONE

Aladdin

New York   London   Toronto   Sydney   New Delhi

ALADDIN

An imprint of Simon & Schuster Children's Publishing Division
1230 Avenue of the Americas, New York, New York 10020
First Aladdin hardcover edition May 2019
Text copyright © 2019 by Lee Gjertsen Malone
Jacket illustration copyright © 2019 by Andy Smith
For information about special discounts for bulk purchases, please contact
Simon & Schuster Special Sales at 1-866-506-1949 or business@simonandschuster.com.
The Simon & Schuster Speakers Bureau can bring authors to your live event.
For more information or to book an event contact the Simon & Schuster Speakers
Bureau at 1-866-248-3049 or visit our website at www.simonspeakers.com.
Jacket designed by Laura Lyn DiSiena
Interior designed by Tom Daly
The text of this book was set in Excelsior LT Std.
Manufactured in the United States of America 0419 FFG
2 4 6 8 10 9 7 5 3 1
Library of Congress Cataloging-in-Publication Data
Names: Malone, Lee Gjertsen, author. | Title: Camp Shady Crook / by Lee
Gjertsen Malone. | Description: First Aladdin hardcover edition. | New York,
New York : Aladdin, 2019. | Summary: Budding con artists Archie and Vivian
spend a summer at a dilapidated, mismanaged Vermont camp competing to get
whatever they want from their fellow campers.
Identifiers: LCCN 2018050779 (print) | LCCN 2018055405 (eBook) |
ISBN 9781534422285 (eBook) | ISBN 9781534422261 (hc)
Subjects: | CYAC: Camps—Fiction. | Swindlers and swindling—Fiction. |
Conduct of life—Fiction. | Friendship—Fiction. | Humorous stories. |
BISAC: JUVENILE FICTION / Sports & Recreation / Camping &
Outdoor Activities. | JUVENILE FICTION / Social Issues / Friendship. |
JUVENILE FICTION / Humorous Stories.
Classification: LCC PZ7.1.M35 (eBook) | LCC PZ7.1.M35 Cam 2019 (print) |
DDC [Fic]—dc23
LC record available at https://lccn.loc.gov/2018050779

For Judy,
who taught me to love books
1943–2017

ARCHIE DRAKE

Twelve-year-old Archie Drake stepped off the bus and took a long, deep breath. He smelled fresh-cut grass; cedar shingles; that dank, dark odor of the lake; and at the very edges of it all, a little bit of campfire.

It was good to be back.

He stepped away from the doorway of the bus to let the other kids pass and gave them his most casual smile.

Already he'd sown the seeds for the first week of camp's Big Game.

It started when his father dropped him off at the strip-mall parking lot, one of the pickup locations for the Camp Shady Brook bus. Camp Shady Brook collected kids every summer from New York City, New Jersey, and Connecticut and drove them deep into New England, where they could spend a week learning archery, water safety, and antiquated campfire songs at a camp nestled into a patch of especially unattractive and straggly woods just outside a completely unremarkable town in Vermont.

A week from now more than half of them would head back on the same bus, with new friends, life-long memories, and more than a few bug bites (the mosquitoes at Shady Brook were notoriously vicious), but without—if Archie's cons worked out, and they usually did—most of their pocket money and small valuables.

Not that it would really matter to them, the way Archie figured it. Most of them had no idea how lucky they were.

Archie had arrived at the mall parking lot in his dad's limo. Well, not actually his dad's, the limo really belonged to Mr. Carvallo, Dad's boss at the car service. Dad just drove it around New Jersey, bringing executives to the airport, teenagers to proms, and brides and grooms to weddings.

As he said good-bye, Archie played it cool, like he didn't want a hug, but that wasn't a problem for his father. Mr. Drake was not a demonstrative man, and he was already late for work. Archie knew how much his dad hated being late.

Once Archie got on the bus, he waved stiffly out the window at his father, who stood next to the door of the limousine in his dark suit and white shirt, his hair slicked back with gel, dark sunglasses shielding his eyes. "Good-bye, Jameson!" Archie shouted at the closed window, deliberately loud enough so the kids nearby would turn their heads. "Give Mother and Father my love!"

He knew his dad couldn't hear what he was saying, which was good, since it was complete fiction.

It was also the first step in convincing the kids on the bus he was someone other than he actually was. Because if he was honest with himself—and Archie was as honest with himself as he was with other people, which meant only rarely, and only when there was something in it for him—that was the main draw of camp. The chance to be someone else. Somebody richer. Better. More important. The kind of person who got a ride in a limo because his family could afford it, not because his father drove one as his job.

As different from the kid he was at home as he could possibly be.

Already his dad's attention was glued to the Bluetooth headset in his ear, telling him he needed to get moving and pick up his next client. Probably some rich guy headed to the airport, at this time of day. With barely a nod, Archie's dad got back into the limo and drove away.

The boy sitting behind Archie poked his head

over the seat and looked out the window to see what Archie was shouting at. "Who was that?" he asked.

"Nobody," Archie said with a downward glance, like he was embarrassed to be caught waving. "Just my . . . ride."

A girl across the aisle leaned over and said in a loud and obvious whisper, "Was that guy, like, your chauffeur?"

"What's a chauffeur?" somebody behind her asked. It sounded like one of the little kids. Camp Shady Brook took in campers from ages eight through thirteen.

"It's a driver, somebody who drives people around as a job, dummy," another voice said. "Lots of people have them."

"Super-rich people," still another voice chimed in. "Like celebrities and billionaires."

Archie averted his eyes from the kids who were now staring at him from all the nearby seats. "It's not important," he said, adding, with a touch of false humility he'd practiced over and over in the mirror all through the school year, "Really. I'm just another camper, like all of you. My name's Archibald Drake the Third, but most people just call me Archie."

A murmur traveled through the crowd.

This wasn't a surprise to Archie. He knew the effect his name had on people. Most of them would immediately think of the other Archie Drake, the flamboyant chairman of Drake Industries, a regular fixture on TV shows and in newspapers, and one of the richest men in the world. Archie never actually told anyone at camp he was related to that Mr. Drake, and would avoid the question when he was asked directly.

But he also never told people he wasn't.

Six glorious weeks spread out ahead of him. More than a whole month of sunshine and canoeing, but also, if his plans worked out, six weeks of cons and cold, hard cash. Camp Shady Brook required every camper to bring at least fifty dollars of pocket money to spend at the camp store, a fact Archie had learned to exploit his very first summer there, two years ago.

He'd never understood why cartoons showed characters with a light bulb hanging in space over their head when they got a big idea, but that day, two years ago, he finally got the metaphor. It had been such a simple con, in retrospect. One of those snobby rich kids he'd been afraid to talk to that summer had offered him money in the camp store, because they thought he was related to the other, more important Archie Drake. He'd been stunned, but the kids had taken his shocked response as false modesty and bought him all the candy bars he'd been drooling over with no cash of his own to spend. Instant respect, and instant benefit, all from an easy-to-understand (and explained away, if that came to it) misunderstanding. The perfect con. And it had fallen into his lap.

That moment had changed his summer—changed his life, even, since from then on he knew he was no longer boring/short/bad-at-sports Archie Drake, whatever the kids at home thought. He was someone else. A master of deception.

And now he was back for more. It was almost like coming home—well, if your version of "home" was the worst summer camp in the entire state of Vermont, perhaps New England.

He glanced around the bus. Each week it would take away a load of campers, sunburned, tired, and poorer. Then it would return with a whole new crop of kids, ready to meet Archie. Or Archibald. Or "A-Man" or "Drake" or whatever other nickname he decided to crown himself with, depending on his mood and scheme. All of those new campers, wandering off the bus each week with their duffel bags and eager smiles. Meek sheep, totally unaware of what was in store. At least until the end of the week, when they'd go home and beg their parents not to send them back to boring and beat-up Camp Shady Brook—or as he liked to think of it, Camp Shady Crook—ever again.

VIVIAN CHENG

Camp. Stupid, dumb, boring camp. Bugs all over the place and wearing sunscreen every day even when it wasn't sunny and sleeping in a cabin with a ton of random girls who would probably end up hating her instead of staying at home in her room or traveling to some awesome hotel on one of her parents' swanky summer trips.

Vivian was not happy. She loved summer in the city, even though the streets smelled like three-day-old garbage and the glare off the pavement made it impossible to see anything even through her nicest pair of sunglasses. She loved hanging out in her apartment building's lobby with Margot, who lived upstairs, going to Central Park to people-watch, and poking through Duane Reade to get some air-conditioning and maybe some new glitter nail polish. Convincing tourists in Penn Station they were stuck without train fare and just needed fifteen dollars to get home to New Jersey—even though the only times she'd been to New Jersey were when she and her parents flew out of Newark airport.

The airport. Vivian didn't even want to think about it. Airports meant flying and travel and all sorts of fun, exciting adventures. Adventures that involved elegant hotels and five-star restaurants in places like Hong Kong, not whatever was going to pass for meals and sleeping accommodations in Middle of Nowheresville, Vermont.

Vivian's parents owned a specialty travel agency that catered to the wealthiest world travelers. In the summer they took their richest clients on fancy trips to the most exciting destinations in Asia—and in past years Vivian always got to come along. But thanks to some . . . issues that had developed this year at school, that wasn't in the cards. Not this summer.

"We think you need more supervision," her mother had said, standing in her favorite crisp plum-colored suit in the kitchen of their Manhattan apartment earlier that year. "Your father and I can't watch you every second. Camp would be a . . . better experience for you."

Better how? Vivian thought. Instead of exploring the Yangtze River on a luxury riverboat—this summer's first planned excursion—she'd be eating twigs and berries and singing ridiculous songs around a campfire, batting away mosquitoes with a bunch of mouth-breathers from the suburbs. For six whole weeks.

She'd rather go to prison. At least in prison they had TV.

"I can't believe you're doing this to me! It's like I'm being punished for something that wasn't even really my fault," she said, appealing to her father, who sat at the little kitchen table in the corner looking at his laptop. "Won't you miss me?" She gave him the Look, which usually worked. Dad was a soft touch.

"Of course we'll miss you, sweetheart," he said with a sad smile. "But it's not fair to our clients if we have to watch you all the time. And we don't want you to get in any more trouble."

"But none of it was my fault," Vivian grumbled.

"What was that?" her mother asked.

"Nothing," Vivian replied, and heaved a huge sigh. She didn't know how to explain what had really happened at school that year, especially since she was sure they would never understand. How do you explain to your parents that you've failed utterly and miserably at being a normal kid? How do you explain to your parents that you can't even make friends? Not real friends, anyway. It was better to just act like she didn't care.

But things began to look up on the bus when she met some of the other kids headed to Camp Shady Brook.

Well, not at first. Her seatmate had irritated her right from the minute she opened her mouth. "I'm Sasha Howard! I'm from White Plains! This is my first time at Camp Shady Brook, but I'm so excited! I've never been to camp before!"

Every sentence sounded like it ended in an exclamation point. Or, as Vivian soon learned, a question mark. And obviously this girl wanted to be friends. But she didn't know Vivian. She didn't know that Vivian didn't do "friends" anymore. Not after last year.

"Do you think it's going to be fun there? I don't know if I'll like the food? Or if they have private showers?" The girl let out a high-pitched self-conscious giggle.

Vivian didn't even want to contemplate the idea of nonprivate showers. What was this place, stuck in the Dark Ages?

Finally the girl took a breath. "Oh my God, I'm talking so much! I'm so sorry! I'm just soooooo excited! What's your name and where are you from?"

"Vivian Cheng," Vivian said, blowing her shaggy bangs off her forehead in irritation. The bus was air-conditioned, but barely, and unlike the rest of the kids in their shorts and tank tops, she was wearing skinny jeans and her favorite tall black leather boots. "And I live in Lenox Hill."

"Where's that?" Sasha asked. "Long Island?"

Vivian frowned, and her tone became even icier. "The Upper. East. Side. Of MANHATTAN."

"Oooooh!" Sasha said. "I love the city! My dad works there! We go there all the time! For our class trip we went to the Museum of Natural History!"

Vivian rolled her eyes and tried to look out the window to get away from the girl's beaming face. She always felt awkward around aggressively friendly people. People who acted like they were from another planet where everybody was nice and happy. She just knew she was destined to be the first person to disappoint them.

Finally Sasha seemed to notice her reluctance to talk.

"I'm sorry, are you shy? That's okay, I'm shy too? Sometimes?" she said, and then paused. "You know what, there are some kids from my school on this bus! I can introduce you! Then you'll know lots of people at camp! It'll be great!"

To Vivian's horror, Sasha stood up and started calling out names like an extremely happy drill sergeant calling role. "Aidan! Phoebe! Lily!" she sung out. "This is Vivian! She's from New York City!"

Vivian slid down lower in her seat.

One of the girls Sasha had called over—Vivian

hadn't caught her name—gave a sour look. "What's so special about New York City? My dad works for a company that's based in France and we go to Paris all the time."

"I've been to Paris," Vivian said suddenly. And she had—it was the jumping-off point of a tour for European clients her parents had organized two summers ago. The group had met in Paris and then flown to Vietnam.

The sour-faced girl looked skeptical, but the other kids were rapt, so Vivian kept going, even though she normally wouldn't be talking this much. It was so rare to feel like people were actually interested in what she had to say. Even before everything had gone upside down, her former best friend, Margot, usually acted like she was just waiting for Vivian to finish so she could start talking. "I've been a lot of places, actually. My parents own a travel agency. We go to China, Korea, Thailand, Vietnam . . . all over Asia. And other places, too."

"Wow," one of the kids breathed. "My dad's parents are from Korea but I've never been there. He says it's too expensive."

"Korea's amazing," Vivian said, turning toward the boy. "If you go, you have to go to Jeju Island. It's gorgeous there."

And that's how it all started. At first, she'd only begun talking because she wanted to wipe that smirk off the face of Little Miss I Went to Paris. But pretty quickly she found herself enjoying all the attention of the rest of the campers on the bus, and began to tell them some of the best stories of her world travels. Most of the stories she told were true, but as she continued, she realized she could literally tell them anything and they would believe her. Why wouldn't they? She sounded like she knew what she was talking about. And they had no clue who she really was.

For a tiny instant, she wondered if it might be nice to make friends with some of these kids, at least for the summer. A chance to start over. But she pushed that thought deep down. She sucked at making friends, so there was no point in even trying. If she'd learned anything at all in the past year, she'd learned that.

Instead a brand-new idea began to form. A plan to have a little fun—with kids who probably weren't going to like her anyway once they got to camp. If she could convince them she was a world traveler, maybe she could convince them to do stuff for her, just like those tourists in Penn Station. And just like Margot had done to her, last year, when she pretended to be her friend.

Which might mean Camp Shady Brook wasn't going to be that bad after all.

ARCHIE

Archie first started going to Camp Shady Brook three years before, when his stepmom, Alicia, had the twins. The twins were "a handful," as Archie's dad put it, so it "made more sense" for him not to be "stuck at home" for the whole summer. Almost the minute Archie's dad said those words Alicia produced a glossy brochure with a picture of a cabin nestled in a beautiful forest on the front and an application for financial aid for needy campers.

"This place looks great," she gushed. "And they want some kids there on scholarship or something, so we wouldn't even have to pay for him to go. For six weeks!" She seemed annoyingly overjoyed at the prospect of shipping him off to another state. Alicia was okay, most of the time, but she had trouble pretending that she consid-

ered Archie anything more than a burden, especially after the twins were born. It was hard not to
feel displaced, whatever people said.

Archie's dad had nodded too fast and too enthu-
siastically for Archie to have any hope of changing his mind. It was obvious Dad and Alicia had
hatched this plan together as a way to get him out
of their hair for most of the summer.

At first Archie was incensed they were sending him away to summer camp. And for six whole
weeks—most of the kids in his neighborhood either
went to day camp at the YMCA or, if they were
really lucky, away for a week or two to learn soccer
or karate. Not off to Vermont for most of summer
vacation. "Why don't you guys ship me off to mili-
tary school?" he protested. "Then you could get rid
of me for the whole year, not just the summer."

"We're not trying to get rid of you, Archie," his
dad had said. But his tone, to Archie, was uncon-
vincing. It was just difficult to picture Dad being all
that interested in another summer with a kid who
hated barbeque and ball sports (both on TV and in
real life)—his dad's two summer passions—when
he had a new wife, and two new kids, to be excited
about. But that was a thought that Archie would
have keeled over and died before expressing to anyone, especially his father. "We just want you to try
something new. And maybe even have some fun."

Archie arrived at camp that first summer extremely skeptical he would have any fun at all. He was on edge from the very first minute, convinced that everything from his cheap backpack to his hand-me-down clothes were practically a billboard screaming *Charity Case!* But it only took a day or two into the first week of his very first year at Shady Brook to realize the multitude of opportunities that lay in front of him.

For one thing, nobody knew who he was. Not like at home, where everyone knew his mom had skipped out when Archie was five and that his dad drove a limo and his stepmother ran the worst nail salon in town. She could paper the walls with the health code violations she'd racked up. Her Yelp reviews—Archie had checked—read like a script for a horror movie about a serial killer who attacked her victims with cuticle scissors.

Not only did all the kids at home know full well that he wasn't related to the wealthy Archibald Drake, back in Trenton it was plain he was about as far removed from that kind of life as one kid could possibly be. At home he didn't fit in anywhere. Not at school, where the kids only cared about whether or not you were good at sports and video games, and not in his neighborhood, where they only cared whether or not you could beat people up. And since Archie could do none of those things, he was at best completely invisible. At worst, he spent half his time walking around with a bright red bull's-eye on his back.

But at camp—at camp people didn't know the limo driver was his dad. They didn't know that the other Mr. Drake wasn't his uncle (or his father, or his grandfather—he never said anything concrete, but the campers all had their theories). All they knew was what he told them. And, he realized a few days into his deception, being able to be anything he wanted also meant that he could persuade some of them—not all of them, but enough—to do anything he wanted. Mainly, to give him things. Candy from their care packages (Archie's dad and stepmom always said they would send care packages but somehow never managed to pull them together in time). Various goodies purchased at the camp store. And, unbelievably, money. So many of these kids had more than they could ever appreciate, and Archie began to feel like it was his personal mission to get them to share their undeserved wealth—well, except for the other scholarship kids, but he could usually pick them out pretty easily. By the time he got home, he was already begging to go back the following summer. Another chance to be someone completely different from who he was at home.

And now he was back for a third year. And it was going to be his best yet.

As Archie walked toward the main building, where they would have camp orientation—after they gave out bunk assignments, the counselors would sing a few silly songs, then the camp director would quickly launch into an extended list of rules Archie already planned to ignore—he heard a noise.

A girl was talking, loudly and nervously. But what really caught Archie's attention was his very strong impression that she was . . . faking.

As a notorious faker himself, he could spot another one a mile away.

"Oh my gawd, I am having the. Worst. Day. Ever," the girl was saying to the group clustered around her. "I can't believe I forgot we were supposed to pack a lunch for the bus! And now they're saying we won't eat again until dinner! And I was in too much of a hurry this morning and I didn't eat any breakfast . . ." She looked forlorn. The girl wore a black T-shirt with the name of a band Archie had never heard of, and her long hair was cut in a shaggy style like a teenager, though she was only about his age. Instead of shorts, she wore dark jeans and boots. She seemed cool and collected, except for her face, which was on the verge of tears.

One of the girls near her piped up. "Hey, you know, I could share with you if you want. My mother sent me with a bunch of cupcakes. They're for the whole week, but if you're really hungry . . ."

"Oh, no, I couldn't take your food," the girl was saying loudly, but she was already poking through the box the other girl had held out, pulling out two cupcakes and stuffing one in her mouth. "Thanks!" she said over her shoulder as she walked off past Archie. "I mean it. You're the best."

And as she sauntered past, eating her cupcake, for a brief second he swore he saw her wink.

Uh-oh, he thought.

Competition.

VIVIAN

Vivian had already begun to come up with the first steps of her plan by the time they reached the old, beat-up camp, which was stuck at the end of a long and dusty dirt road and looked like a home for delinquents, not a place people would send children they actually hoped to see come back healthy and happy at the end of the summer.

Well, at least she had a vague idea of how she could make this all work out in her favor, if she wasn't going to "have fun" or "make friends" like her parents had oh-so-helpfully instructed her to do before she left.

Instead, she decided it was her turn to be in control. Vivian knew in her heart she was more capable than any of those stupid people at school believed.

She tried her first little ploy on a group of girls

who had gotten off another bus, probably from Connecticut or New Jersey or someplace like that. Two of the girls looked admiringly at her outfit as she approached, so they seemed like the perfect test. And they were—that one girl was bragging so much about the fancy cupcakes she'd brought from home it seemed only right to make her give some of them up. To Vivian, naturally.

This might work out just fine, Vivian thought as she walked past an odd-looking boy wearing a perfectly ironed button-down shirt and impossibly tidy khaki shorts. He looked more like someone who worked in a bank than a camper.

She pushed down deep inside the vague feeling of guilt at how easy it was to get those cupcakes away from that girl. It was just a game, anyway. A little lark.

Because nobody here wanted to be her friend. She knew that. So she wasn't going to feel bad about taking advantage of them. She'd learned that the hard way, last year at school. It was a tough world—you either eat or you get eaten. Or, at least, your cupcakes do.

The strange boy looked away from her, like he'd been eavesdropping on her conversation. But she didn't really care. Wasn't that her new mantra? She didn't care about any of them. So instead she gave him a sly wink as she walked past and wondered what she could get a boy like that to do for her. He seemed like the sort of kid who might be an easy target.

"Hey," the boy said. She ignored him and sped up, heading toward the main building, where they were supposed to meet their counselors. But, annoyingly, he kept pace behind her. "Hey," he said again.

She turned around and tossed her hair. "What do you want?"

"It's just that—it's just that, we're not supposed to have food from home once we get off the bus. Especially not in the cabins," he said, stepping closer. His hair was cut supershort, like a Marine recruit, and he had one of those wide, nervous smiles. "Care packages are supposed to be kept in the mess hall. Because of bugs and stuff. I read about it in the handbook."

"Like I care," she said. She took another big bite of cupcake.

"Well, okay, but that other girl who gave it to you is gonna get in trouble if they find out what she has, and if she gets in trouble, then you're going to get in trouble. They are really, really strict here. You don't want to put a toe out of line, trust me. I heard the camp director is the meanest in the entire state of Vermont."

Vivian frowned at him. "Maybe you worry about stuff like that, but I don't."

"Well, you should," he said. He paused, and then added, "Especially if your plan is to scam girls out of their snacks."

Vivian stared at him for a minute, surprised. How did he know she'd been lying?

"I'm Archie," he said, sticking out his hand. She ignored it and kept chewing. "And I'm just trying to give you a heads-up! This isn't that sort of camp where you can get away with anything. You really have to follow the rules. I heard people get sent home for a lot less than a couple of cupcakes! Shady Brook isn't like Camp Hiawatha across the lake, or Northern Star in New Hampshire—you can get away with all sorts of craziness at those places. But not here." He glanced around, like armed riot police would descend any second for even just discussing the possibility of breaking camp rules. "I'm actually a little scared. My parents said it cost a lot of money to go here. I don't know what they'll do to me if I get kicked out!"

Vivian frowned again, but this time at the ground, not at the strange boy. Unfortunately, he didn't seem like the kind of person who would lie, not about something like this. Were there really that many rules and regulations here at Shady Brook? Maybe this camp wasn't going to be the free-for-all she'd expected.

Her parents had said the whole point of going to

camp was that she needed more supervision. Maybe they'd picked Shady Brook for exactly that reason, and this kid was right about the rules. The same six weeks still stretched out ahead of her, but now they were filled with boring Goody Two-shoes kids who always colored inside the lines in art class and never, ever stayed up past lights out. Like some sort of nerd jail.

I have to get out of here, she thought. But she knew getting in trouble and getting kicked out wouldn't help; her parents would just find another place to send her, and the next place would probably be worse. They'd been clear that she needed to be watched, after all.

She sighed and gave the boy a half smile. He had dropped his hand but still looked at her expectantly. "Well, thanks for the info, I guess," she said, and began to walk away.

As she left the boy smiled back at her. But there was something distinctly odd about his smile. He seemed almost . . . pleased with himself. It was the way Margot smiled when they had pulled off another stunt at school, before Margot had gotten expelled and Vivian had gotten a three-day suspension. Before she'd figured out that she'd been played all along by someone she thought was her friend. It wasn't something she wanted to dwell on. She'd learned her lesson the hard way, and being at some dumb camp wasn't going to change her mind.

But of course, a guy like this wasn't doing anything other than trying to be a Good Citizen, and telling her she needed to follow the rules or Face the Consequences. What could he possibly be pleased about, except helping a fellow camper get with the program? She shook the thought out of her head and gave him a half-hearted wave. "See you around."

ARCHIE

Archie couldn't stop smiling as the girl walked away. He wondered if she'd hurry off to her bunk to write to her parents and beg them to switch her to one of those other camps he'd mentioned—or if she'd just spend her time at Shady Brook carefully following the rules, leaving all the good targets to him. Either way, like most of the campers, she'd be gone in a week, long before she figured out that despite all the regulations at Camp Shady Brook, there were still plenty of opportunities for a kid as savvy as he was.

"What was that all about?" a low voice said over his shoulder. Archie spun around and found himself face-to-face with a large boy, probably only about fifteen years old but built like he was far older. He was wearing a bulky hooded sweatshirt that looked too heavy for the warm summer weather, with the hood up, and the kind of baggy cargo shorts that seemed to only stay up as if by magic. "Causing trouble already, Drake?"

"No," Archie said, loud enough for the kids milling around to hear. "I'm just waiting for my luggage to come off the bus, like everyone else, Oliver."

"And bothering the new girls," the boy sneered. "Why don't you do them all a favor and keep away from them this summer? They're supposed to be here to see the beautiful wilderness, not your ugly face."

By now a bunch of the kids who had been on Archie's bus had gathered around, staring at the confrontation. But none of them seemed to want to come too close to the little scene that was playing out just out of earshot of the adults who were overseeing the unloading of the buses.

Archie took a deep breath. "You know, Oliver, if you keep bothering me I'll be forced to talk to Ms. Hess. I don't want to do it, but you leave me no choice."

"'You leave me no choice,'" Oliver said in a mocking baby voice. "I can't get over the way you talk, Drake, it's hilarious." He reached out and gave Archie a not-so-playful shove.

"Don't touch me," Archie said, but his voice wavered. Then, standing up straighter, he said more firmly, "You'll regret it, Oliver. I'm not putting up with this stuff anymore, not this summer."

Archie reached out and grabbed Oliver's sweatshirt, and got up close—right in his face, even
though he had to look way up to see into the eyes
of the larger kid. The audience surrounding them
gasped. Was this going to be an actual fight? Just
minutes after they'd all gotten off the buses from
home? Where were the counselors? Why wasn't anyone interfering?

Despite all the people watching, nobody noticed
the small slip of paper that Archie tucked in the
pocket of Oliver's sweatshirt. It was a note, sharing the details of their first meeting that night during "Quiet Time" after dinner. But of course, their
audience had no idea that they weren't enemies,
not at all.

Because that was the whole point of this little
charade.

Oliver reared back from Archie's touch like he
was going to tackle the smaller boy, then deflated
when he spotted one of the counselors coming
around the side of the building toward the mass of
campers. Archie pushed back a smile as he walked
away. He was looking forward to meeting up with
Oliver. It wasn't something he would admit to anyone (least of all Oliver) but the boy who looked like
the camp bully to everyone else was the closest
thing he had to a friend, either here or at home.

"Hey, time to grab your gear and get your bunk assignment!" the counselor called, in that cheery, first-day-of-camp voice they all used. Archie didn't know this counselor, but that wasn't unusual. Shady Brook rarely had counselors—or campers—return for a second summer. He suspected working there was probably almost as bad as attending. Maybe even worse, since you had to deal with Ms. Hess as your boss and not just as the camp director. He sometimes shuddered to think what she would be like if she was paying your salary, instead of cashing your parents' checks.

What most of them didn't realize yet was that Camp Shady Brook was far from the beautiful idyll pictured on its brochures. That's because most of the camp's budget was actually spent *on* the brochures, which were admittedly magnificent—thick, glossy paper covered in photos of model-perfect children engaged in all sorts of fun activities. The director, Philomena Hess (usually called "Miss Hiss" by most of the campers and about half the staff), hired an ad agency to put it together at great expense. "Marketing is very important" is what she told the camp's owners, an elderly couple named Mr. and Mrs. Beaumont, who rarely made it out to visit the camp anymore, much less get involved in the day-to-day activities. The Beaumonts had run the camp for years, until health problems had forced them to pass on the reins to a new director.

Miss Hiss used to be in charge of a whole chain of camps all throughout New England, until she was fired for reasons the campers, at least, did not understand. But her office was filled with awards she'd won in her last job, and pictures of her shaking hands with various elected officials.

But those days were behind her. Now she was the director of arguably the worst camp in Vermont, and she appeared to be personally committed to making it worse by the minute.

Truth was, Camp Shady Brook was a con bigger than anything Archie had ever come up with.

There wasn't even a real brook, despite the name. The lake was fed by a man-made channel lined in concrete, and choked with weeds and sludge. It was about as close to a "shady brook" as a trip to the dentist was to Disney World.

(Archie knew the name was a marketing choice, made after Ms. Hess discovered that the lovely-sounding Native American name the Beaumont family had picked for their camp years ago from the local Abenaki language actually meant "Stranger go home.")

The smiling counselor called out again to the crowd of kids, and Oliver melted away as the rest of the campers shuffled toward the pile of luggage and sleeping bags that had been thrown haphazardly in the dirt in front of the camp office.

A boy who had been on Archie's bus came up beside him and leaned in to ask quietly, "Who was that guy?"

"Oh, that's Oliver, he's a CIT," Archie said with a grim face. "Counselor-in-training—they help out with the younger kids," he added by way of explanation. "But you really don't want to get on his bad side, if you know what I mean. I made that mistake last summer." He shuddered theatrically. It was at least partially true—two years ago, Oliver had caught Archie in one of his cons. What the boy didn't know was that instead of turning him in, Oliver had become his partner in crime. And the closest thing he had to a real friend, but again, that wasn't the type of thought Archie would ever share.

The boy gulped and nodded. This time Archie didn't allow himself to smile, but internally he was grinning. At camp less than half an hour and he'd put off that cupcake girl as competition, arranged his first meeting with Oliver, and set in motion a couple of potential cons. Not bad for the first day. Not bad at all.

VIVIAN

Vivian was completely and totally bummed out. After weeks of dreading camp, she'd only just begun to convince herself on the bus there might be some benefit to being here. Finally she could be the one running things, not just the little lackey, like she'd been at school with Margot before she got blamed for everything that happened. But now, thanks to that boy's warnings, those hopes were dashed.

It figured. She never should have let herself get excited. Being enthusiastic about stuff only ever ended badly for her.

As she approached the pile of luggage she considered her options—all dismal. She could call her parents and beg them to let her come home, but she strongly doubted complaining that the camp was too strict would do her any good.

She could try to break enough rules to get kicked out, but that came with risks too. If she got shipped home then they'd just find another camp to send her to—they weren't going to take her to China, especially not if she got in trouble yet again. Vivian wasn't the kind of person who normally had regrets, but this year, she definitely had a few.

"There really has to be a better system for this," she said to no one in particular as she shoved past a slow-moving nine-year-old to reach her own black rolling bag, which she spotted near the back of the enormous, disorganized pile.

"Yeah! I know! Totally!" a voice said from behind her. Vivian's heart sank. "Oh, hi! It's you again!" the voice said.

"Hi," Vivian said, without turning around. She already knew who it was.

"It's me! Sasha from the bus! Did you get your bunk assignment yet? You're going into seventh grade, right? I think all the girls from seventh are in the same cabin? Which maybe means we are bunking together? That would be awesome!"

"Maybe," Vivian said. She clamored over a small girl who was laid out flat on her back in the dust panting from the effort of trying to find her stuff, and sidestepped two boys who were shoving each other in a heated dispute over a sleeping bag. Counselors stood around the huge pile with clipboards like scientists watching a horde of hungry jackals trying to attack an elephant. And behind them all, pacing back and forth, was a woman with the fiercest expression and the biggest clipboard Vivian had ever seen.

Just the sight of her scowling at the campers grappling for their luggage was enough to make even the most self-confident kid's blood run cold.

Vivian didn't know it yet, but that was Ms. Hess (better known as Miss Hiss) the camp director, and she wasn't happy. Then again—and Vivian didn't know this, either—Miss Hiss was rarely happy. It was one of the reasons why so few campers ever returned to Shady Brook, once they filled their parents in on what really went on there. Those who did return were usually the kids who had few, if any, other options. You could see their resigned faces here and there as they trooped off the bus, little pockets of gloom amid the excited energy of the new campers.

"Okay, campers, gather your things and line up to get your bunk assignment and to hand in all electronic devices, including cameras! Come on, people! This shouldn't take all day," Miss Hiss bellowed over the throng of voices rising from the shoving, clamoring children.

The kids who already had their luggage snapped to attention and began to line up. Miss Hiss had one of those voices that demanded to be obeyed.

But there was one boy who seemed oblivious to the shouting camp director—instead he stood perilously close to her, texting on what seemed to be a conspicuously nice phone.

Miss Hiss glared at the boy, and when he still didn't notice her, she marched over, seeming to grow in size as she walked. Around her, small children cowered like they would from an approaching dragon.

"DIDN'T YOU HEAR ME THE FIRST TIME?" she roared right in the texting boy's face. He jumped, and dropped his phone, which fell to the rocky ground with an unfortunate sounding thump.

A slow smile spread across Miss Hiss's face, which only made her look more terrifying, and her voice got lower. The children had stopped collecting their bags and stood in silence so they could hear every word. "You need to get one thing straight, young man. When I speak, you listen. When I say jump, you jump. And when I say HAND OVER YOUR ELECTRONIC DEVICES, you do that without question. Am I perfectly clear?"

The boy gave a sharp, worried-looking nod, but then he couldn't help shooting a quick glance down at the phone that still lay at their feet. Miss Hiss was faster than he was, though, and snatched it up. "Oh, what a shame," she said with fake concern. "Oh dear."

"What happened? Is it broken? Is the screen cracked?" The boy's voice was panicked. "That phone is brand-new!"

Miss Hiss held the phone out of his reach and then, with a quick motion, stuck it in the pocket of her jacket. "I guess you'll need to wait until the last day of camp to find out."

"But that's a whole week away!" the boy pleaded. "Please tell me if it's busted! My mom is going to kill me!"

His words had no effect. Miss Hiss turned away with a satisfied smile and headed back toward the main building, as all around her, kids pulled out electronics from their pockets and bags and handed them over as quickly as possible to the nearest counselor.

Despite the scene that had just played out in front of her, Vivian had no intention of giving up her camera. It was a very nice one her parents had bought her back when they actually trusted her to come on trips with them, and while she was sure there would be nothing worth photographing in this desolate place, she didn't want any of these other kids to get their grubby hands on it. She was glad she'd stowed it safely away in her toiletries kit, deep inside her luggage. She made a mental note to find a good place to hide it once they were allowed into whatever miserable structure would pass as their cabin for the next few weeks.

After the electronics were collected, the counselors began to line up in front of the main building and corral the kids for their cabins. Each counselor had writing on the back of their clipboards, which they held up so the kids could see—*Age Nine Girls*, *Age Nine Boys*, and so on. At the far end of the line was a young, tiny woman, shorter than some of the boys in Vivian's class at school. Her clipboard said *Age Twelve Girls*.

And standing next to her was Sasha-from-the-Bus and two of the other girls Vivian had impressed with her travel stories during the ride—the girls she'd been looking forward to scamming this summer, before that silly boy fouled up everything with his talk of rules and punishments.

Sasha was jumping up and down and waving madly. "Vivian!" she called. "Vivian!" Then, when Vivian didn't wave back, "Vivian?"

Reluctantly Vivian rolled her suitcase over to the group. Might as well get it over with.

"I'm Janet," the tiny counselor-type woman said nervously, slapping at a mosquito that seemed intent on biting her right in the bend of her elbow. "Are you twelve?"

"Yeah," Vivian said.

"Well, okay, then," the woman answered, looking around. She heaved a big sigh, deeper and louder than you would expect from such a tiny person. "I think you're the last one."

She glanced at the ten girls standing around her. "Are you sure you guys are just twelve? You seem . . . bigger than I expected."

"Well, I'm definitely twelve," Vivian said. "My birthday was in March."

For some reason—and it couldn't have been Vivian's tone—Janet smiled at her and added, almost like they were friends, "I've got to say, I wasn't expecting to be assigned to the big kids so soon . . . I thought they'd start me out with the nine-year-olds or something, since I'm new. Oh well. I guess we'll have to make it work."

Little Miss I Went to Paris, who was standing with Sasha, gave a wicked grin and said loudly to the girls standing nearest her, "Well now, ladies. Looks like we got a pushover." Sasha laughed nervously and then looked around to see if anyone had noticed.

Janet must have heard the comment but chose to ignore it. "Okay, I guess we're all here. We should probably head to our cabin. Let's go, Rainbow Smelts!"

All ten girls gaped at her. So she sighed again and said, "Rainbow Smelt is the name of our cabin." Then when the girls kept staring, she added, "The cabins are named after local fish. It's a . . . Camp Shady Brook thing."

Vivian wondered if everything they called "a Camp Shady Brook thing" would be something she'd dislike as much as being known as a Rainbow Smelt. At this point it seemed highly likely.

Janet led the group of twelve-year-old girls away from the ongoing luggage scrum and down a shaded path toward a row of dank cabins that, up close, looked even worse than Vivian had imagined in her darkest daydreams about the horrors that awaited her at summer camp.

Even the normally overexcited Sasha-from-the-Bus seemed to deflate as Janet walked them past all the cabins, each one more run down and moldy than the last, to the final one in the row. "We're supposed to stay . . . here?" Sasha wondered quietly to herself. "Like, all of us? Together?"

"Welcome to your new home for the next week!" Janet said as they all gathered in front of the small, dark building. She spoke loudly, almost too loudly, but without any real enthusiasm. "Let's check it out!"

Janet walked up the rickety steps that protruded from the front of the building like an afterthought and tugged on the door, which was really just a wooden frame with a tattered screen and a thin crosspiece holding it together. As the sad excuse for a door slammed open against the decaying wood exterior of the cabin, one of the hinges popped off and the whole contraption dangled uselessly to the side. "Guess I'll have to get the maintenance staff to fix that," Janet said helplessly, looking at the broken pieces of wood and netting. "Oh well, we should go inside and pick out bunks."

The girls pushed past the broken door and into the dark room. Janet flicked a light switch, and a single unadorned bulb came to life in the middle of the ceiling, emitting barely enough light to show the dark shapes of the bunk beds that circled the cabin.

"I call top bunk!" Sasha-from-the-Bus shouted, running toward a set of bunk beds next to the far window and hoisting her luggage on top. "Lily, come share with me!" she called to Little Miss I Went to Paris, but the girl ignored her and chose a bunk on the opposite side of the room, locking arms with another girl as they marched over to their new bunks together.

"Vivian?" Sasha said, sounding defeated. Vivian reluctantly dragged her suitcase down the aisle between the beds and put it on the bunk Sasha was waving from. Sharing a bunk with Sasha wasn't her top choice, but then again, none of this was even close to being her choice at all.

As she half-heartedly opened up her suitcase, she sighed. If this was just the first day, it was going to be a very long summer.

ARCHIE

rchie's cabin—the twelve-year-old boys were known as the Walleyes, which was only marginally better than being called the Rainbow Smelts—was at the other end of the row from Vivian and the rest of the twelve-year-old girls. Once he'd allowed himself a moment of satisfaction about neutralizing her as a threat, he hadn't given Vivian any thought whatsoever. He had, as the old expression went, bigger fish to fry.

"This place isn't very large," he said quietly to one of the boys near him as their counselor—a peppy guy named Mick who was, like most of the staff, new this summer—led them into their new home.

"I guess your room at home must be twice the size of this place," the boy said back. "You're Archie Drake, right?"

Archie looked from side to side. "How do you know my name?"

The boy laughed. "Let's just say, word gets around. I'm Tyler. I'm from Trenton, New Jersey."

Archie started at the sound of his hometown, but quickly regained his composure. "Trenton? Where's that?"

"South Jersey," the boy said. "Actually, we really live right outside—but nobody's ever heard of my town, so I just usually say Trenton."

"I see," Archie said, and relaxed. Trenton was pretty big, anyway. And if this boy lived in the sub-urbs, he went to a completely different school district. There was no point in worrying. If someone figured out who he was, well, he'd find a way to make that work for him. He was the king of camp cons, after all. "I'm from North Jersey," he said. "Alpine."

Truthfully, he'd never been to Alpine, but accord-ing to the Internet it was one of the most prosperous towns in the state. To Archie even the word "Alpine" sounded like a place rich people lived, the kind of people who went skiing in Switzerland just for fun and said words like "chalet" instead of "cabin." Maybe he should work that one into his vocabulary this summer, if the opportunity arose.

"Nice!" Tyler said. He hoisted his bag up onto a top bunk near the middle of the cabin. "Wanna share? I don't really know anyone here yet."

"That would be great," Archie said, smiling and laying his chocolate-brown leather suitcase on the lower bunk. He'd acquired it last year, thanks to one of his better cons, from one of the many kids who didn't appreciate nice things the way Archie did. With a few well-placed comments, Archie had managed to convince an especially gullible camper that the inexpensive backpack he'd brought from home was a rare, one-of-kind item, made from materials designed by NASA, and that it could turn invisible under certain conditions. It was a long-shot gambit—the kind of con he would only try late into the summer, when he wasn't worried his reputation would be tarnished by a scam gone wrong—but amazingly, it worked, even though the kid he'd conned had to be at least twelve and claimed to go to a magnet school for gifted children in Westchester. A quick trade, and then all Archie had to do was swipe the bag back and then insist, with a hefty amount of fake outrage, it must have turned invisible and been lost somewhere. He ended up with both his old bag and a new, beautiful suitcase. The experience of watching his victim spend the rest of the week feeling around the ground for an invisible backpack was really just a bonus.

Making sure Tyler was still looking, he carefully opened the suitcase, looked inside a few pockets, and then, more frantically, opened each of the pockets a second time, then a third.

He checked his watch—a fake Rolex he'd bought for ten dollars from a guy selling them on a street corner while his class was on a field trip to New York. Then he frowned. "Do you think they'd let me make a phone call?" he asked Tyler nervously. The boy hadn't started unpacking his own stuff, but was just watching Archie go through his little pantomime with the luggage.

The boy scrunched up his shoulders. "Beats me," he said. "They seem pretty strict about stuff like that, but I don't know. Did you forget something at home? Maybe you should tell them it's an emergency?"

Archie frowned again. "Well, I don't want to lie," he said. "But it is a little bit of an emergency." He drummed his fingers on the top of his suitcase, a move he'd picked up from a movie he'd seen on TV last year. "I'm afraid I've forgotten to bring my wallet. I'll have no spending money at all for the whole summer!"

Tyler's eyes lit up. "The famous Archie Drake? With no cash?" He laughed, and gave Archie a small, friendly punch on the arm.

Archie smiled sweetly back at the boy. Already everything was going exactly according to plan.

VIVIAN

After Vivian and the other girls had unpacked their stuff into the tiny wooden crates that passed for shelves in the cabin, they stood around examining the place in an increasingly depressed silence.

Even bubbly Sasha-from-the-Bus seemed at a loss for words.

Besides the bunks and cubbies, there was a small private room off to the side for Janet, and a tiny bathroom with three ancient sinks, one long, cracked mirror, and two shower stalls each covered by a torn and dirty shower curtain with a faded pattern of trees and flowers.

"At least there's private showers?" Sasha-from-the-Bus finally said, but without her usual peppiness. Nobody else said anything at all, though one of the girls made a strangled noise, like she was trying, and failing, to hold back tears.

The brief flurry of unpacking was followed by a tour of the camp, given by a listless Janet. "That's the lake, I guess," she said as they trudged down a sandy path crisscrossed with roots that seemed purposely placed to trip as many people as possible and past a body of water that looked like something that you'd find at a sewage treatment plant, not a summer camp. "And here's the mess hall. And over there is where people do archery? Or something with arrows. And that's a canoe, I think. Or a kayak, maybe. Some kind of boat?"

Finally she led the group into the main activity hall, where they sat on the hard, splintery floor and listened to the camp director and the counselors spell out all the rules of Camp Shady Brook. If Vivian had any hope that boy she'd met was wrong about how strict the place was, it disappeared completely as she listened to the endless list of regulations.

"Don't go in the lake without supervision," Ms. Hess said firmly as she paced back and forth in front of the silent campers. "Don't go in the woods at all. Never go out to the old boathouse, at all, ever. No food in the cabins—we don't want bugs. And lights out is at nine p.m., no exceptions."

Don't do this, don't do that, don't go there, don't go here. It was an impossibly long list of don'ts, and every single infraction got you demerits, which lost you privileges and could only be earned off with chores like cleaning the cabin toilets and washing dishes. If Miss Hiss was telling the truth about her plans for punishments—and Vivian strongly suspected she was—all but the most strictly obedient campers would be spending half their days confined to their cabins without meals.

Vivian finally stopped paying attention. It was all too oppressive to bear.

It wasn't until they were headed toward the mess hall for their first dinner—which Vivian was pretty confident was going to be inedible—that she finally saw a possible path out of her misery.

Mia, one of the girls in her bunk, was walking near her as they entered the large dining room that sat right next to the main activity hall. It was just as dusty and dilapidated as the rest of the camp, but filled with long wooden tables and low benches, under an arching wood ceiling that even from far below Vivian could tell was full of spiderwebs. She repressed a shiver.

At the end of the room, a group of teenagers was standing behind a counter wearing aprons and hairnets and looking like they'd rather be doing anything else but serving a bunch of younger kids. Vivian really couldn't blame them.

One of them, a big guy with floppy hair and a

hooded gray sweatshirt, looked like his only pleasure in life was spitting in people's food. It took
only a quick glance at him before Vivian decided to
get in the other food line.

"Oh, is that him?" Mia said to no one in particular as she came up behind Vivian.

Vivian didn't say anything at all, but Mia pressed
on. "I think it is! I think it is him!"

Vivian took a deep breath. "Who?" she asked,
since that was obviously what Mia wanted. She
hoped she wasn't talking about the big dude with
the grim smile ladling out dark brown glop onto
plastic plates. The less said about him, the better.

The girl turned, her eyes shining. "Didn't you
hear?" she asked in a low whisper.

"Obviously not," Vivian replied. "Since I have no
idea what you're talking about."

"Archie Drake is here! At Shady Brook!" Mia
said. And then, when Vivian didn't offer a glimmer
of recognition: "*The* Archie Drake?"

The name sounded vaguely familiar, but Vivian
didn't know why. "Okay, Archie Drake is here. And
I should care about this because?"

"Because he's, like, the son of the richest man on
the planet, that's why," the other girl said. "I heard
he's been coming here for years. And that his parents might even own this place, though then I heard
he said that wasn't true. But his parents own, like,

everything. All I know is, I never imagined I'd go to summer camp with Archie Drake!"

As she spoke, Mia poked Vivian in the arm, and then pointed toward a table on the other side of the room. Vivian looked over, bored, but then her head snapped back to look again.

"Don't stare," Mia hissed.

But Vivian couldn't help herself. That rich kid Mia was talking about? The one whose parents "owned everything" and probably owned Camp Shady Brook, too? She stared for a long minute, shaking her head.

It was that awkward boy who had convinced her that having cupcakes in her cabin would be treated like an act of high treason. The kid who said it was his first summer of camp, and that his parents would be mad if he got kicked out because camp cost too much money.

But he didn't look awkward or unsure of himself anymore. Instead he sat with a wide smile, surrounded by admirers hanging on his every word.

"Oh, right," Vivian said, half to Mia, but more to herself. "That Archie Drake."

ARCHIE

After dinner, when the campers were supposed to go back to their cabin to get cleaned up and "rest" (Camp Shady Brook code for "Be quiet and stay out of everyone's hair for an hour") in preparation for the Saturday night bonfire, Archie slipped out of the Walleyes' cabin undetected and headed for the small wooded area behind the archery range. The woods were off-limits but Archie knew which parts of the camp were regularly patrolled and which ones weren't. It was one of the many useful bits of information he'd gleaned during previous summers.

Oliver was already waiting, and Archie quickly filled him in on the day's events—including his encounter with the wannabe con artist, Cupcake Girl.

"I don't see why you bother with a kid like

that; there's no way she'd ever be real competition," Oliver said. "Scamming a couple of cupcakes? That's preschool-level stuff."

"You don't understand, Oliver," Archie said patiently. "Once a girl like that starts manipulating people, feelings will get hurt, and all our little sheep will get nervous. Or worse, they'll go to the counselors. Then we'll have no luck at all."

Oliver laughed. "Only newbies would go to the counselors at Shady Brook." It took only a few days before people realized that bringing anything to the attention of the staff at camp only ended up getting you into trouble yourself. The counselors—and especially Miss Hiss—hated complainers more than they hated troublemakers, a situation Archie had used to his advantage more than once.

"But isn't that the point?" Archie said. "Most of them *are* newbies, and we both know better than to try anything with the kids who have been here before. And I just don't want a girl like that causing problems for us before we even get started. It's only the first day!"

Oliver nodded slowly, though he didn't seem fully sure.

"Anyway, I've been working on this summer's strategy," Archie said, warming up to the subject. He felt like himself again, back at Camp Shady Crook, scheming with Oliver. It was as if his life at home was actually the fake life, while being here at camp, pretending to be someone else, was who he really was. "I think this week we're going to do the usual, and get them thinking I'm related to the other Archie Drake. Just lay the groundwork for a couple of days, before we get into some of the more complicated stuff. I'll need a loan—my parents forgot to send me money—but I'll pay them back twice what I borrow once I get home. . . . Do that with enough kids and we'll be raking it in by the time they all get on the bus back to their fancy suburbs."

"That's my favorite con," Oliver said, seeming to forget their disagreement about Cupcake Girl now that images of cold, hard cash were dancing in his head. "So simple, yet so effective."

"The best ones usually are," Archie agreed. "There's already one kid in my bunk who's practically panting to give me his cash. Though he obviously thinks he's going to get something in return . . . I am the 'famous Archie Drake,' after all."

They both laughed, and again Archie felt that surge of happiness. It was good to be back.

"His name's Tyler," Archie continued. "He's the perfect candidate for my first mark."

"Our first mark," Oliver said, giving Archie a pointed grin.

There was a crunching sound behind them in the trees, and they both turned to look.

And out stepped Cupcake Girl.

Oliver stepped in front of Archie. "Hey! You're out of bounds. You're not supposed to be out of your cabin during rest period," he demanded in his best tough-guy voice. "What do you think you're doing?"

She gave them both a wide smile. "Eavesdropping, of course. I think your friend Archie here knows all about it. It's—what's the phrase?—'so simple, yet so effective.'"

The two boys stared, open-mouthed. The girl kept walking, deliberately slowly, until she was standing right in front of them with her hands on her hips, blocking their way back to the cabins.

"Okay," Archie said, thinking. "You do know that you get demerits for being out of your bunk, right? So even if you turn us in, you'll get in trouble too. Probably more trouble, actually, since Oliver here is a CIT and so he's allowed to be out and around if it's on camp business, and if he said he was taking me to the infirmary for a stomachache, the camp director might not even give me anything more than a warning."

He smiled back at her, the exact same knowing smile she had given them. "So maybe you should reconsider before you do anything you'll regret."

But the girl's grin didn't dim at his words. "I'm sure the camp director—Ms. Hess, right?—will be way more interested in hearing about your plan to cheat students out of money than about me being out of my bunk. Heck, the look on her face when I explain what you guys are planning might actually be worth a few demerits. Besides, I don't care if I get kicked out. I'm only here for one week, anyway. And right now that feels like a century."

"No," Oliver said, shaking his head back and forth vigorously. "No, no, no."

Oliver would never admit it to anyone, but he was deathly afraid of Miss Hiss.

Archie put up his hand again to silence him. But his smile had disappeared. "So you overheard what we said, and it intrigued you. Okay, I get that," he said. "But if all you wanted was to get us in trouble, you wouldn't have bothered to stop and have this little chitchat—you would have run straight for the main office to tattle before we could stop you. Why don't you just tell us what you want?"

"I want to learn," Vivian said simply.

"Learn?" Oliver asked. "Learn what? Archery?" He snorted.

"No, not archery. And not diving or canoeing or orienteering. I want to learn how to do what you do," she said, looking straight into Archie's eyes. "I thought I was good at convincing people to do stuff back in New York, but this kind of thing— pretending to be a millionaire's son! Getting people to practically beg to give you their money! That's incredible. I mean it. And I don't compliment people all that often, you should know," she added with a toss of her shaggy hair. "The point is, I want to know all your secrets."

"Ha," Archie said. "You don't have any idea who you're dealing with. Do you really think that I'm going to tell you everything I know just because you threatened to tell on me?"

Vivian flicked her hair off her shoulders with one hand and cocked her head at him. "Yes, actually, I do." And then she walked off, so pleased with herself they could almost see the aura of self-satisfaction around her head.

Oliver was extremely skeptical as he and Archie walked back to the cabins. "I don't think you should teach this girl anything. You can't," he said. "Let's come up with another idea—maybe scare her? Something with ghosts. It's easy to convince people there are ghosts around this dump—everything creaks and half the doors open without anyone touching them. Or maybe we should make her think she'll get in real trouble if she works with us? Like, kicked out or something."

"I already tried that with the cupcakes, and it didn't work," Archie said. "And now she knows that she won't get in trouble because she's already figured out that we never get in trouble. And she assumes that if we teach her what we know, she'll be fine."

His mind was racing, but he tried to stay calm, for Oliver's sake. "The only problem is, she's not wrong."

Oliver grumbled something unintelligible.

"I think our best bet is to stick with her like glue all week, and just give her some pointers along the way. She's only here for one week, right? She said that. We could even use her as a pawn in our own cons—then part as friends when the bus comes to pick her up on Saturday," Archie continued. "That way she won't tell on us, and she won't hurt us, either. If she starts making trouble it will ruin everything for the whole summer. I can't stand the idea of Miss Hiss finding out what we're up to. I mean, it's still only the first week of camp."

"Okay, fine, you're the expert," Oliver said, though he still didn't sound fully convinced. "I'd still be getting money out of kids by threatening to punch them in the teeth if it wasn't for you. But just so you know, I don't trust that girl one bit. You need to be careful." He lowered his voice, and added with emphasis, "We both need to be careful."

"I'm always careful," Archie said with his trademark wide smile. "A week from now we'll be cheerily waving at her while she rides the bus home, safe and secure in the knowledge that everything she knows is leaving too. And then the real fun can begin. Heck, if we play our cards right, we might even get to con *her*."

VIVIAN

Vivian knew Archie was in agony at the very idea of teaching her all his tricks. But she could ruin everything for him if she wanted. She'd overheard more than enough.

A guy like that was smart enough to realize when he'd been had. And she'd definitely won this round, she could tell. She was a city kid, after all. She could handle a wannabe from New Jersey. Especially one who claimed to be an expert con artist but couldn't even tell she was lying through her teeth when she said she was leaving Camp Shady Brook in a week. He had no idea she was there for the whole summer. Convincing him of that—you might even call it her first successful con. The thought made her smile more than she had since she'd stepped onto the camp bus. Especially because the girls in her cabin already thought she was the cool New York chick. That was something she could definitely work with.

Archie might think he was so smart, but she was even smarter. And she wasn't going to let some junior level con artist ruin her entire summer.

Finally she was beginning to feel like she was getting her mojo back, after so many months of doubts. All that trouble at school—well, it had been almost more than she could handle, though she would never admit that to anyone, not to her parents and especially not to her so-called best friend, Margot. Even though most of it had been Margot's idea in the first place, changing grades on the school computer. Vivian never would have done any of that, if she hadn't been so desperate for Margot's approval. But at least she'd learned that caring what other kids thought of her only led to heartbreak.

Anyway, that whole mess was behind her now. And this Archie character? Vivian was more than prepared to handle him. She just needed to learn his secrets first. And then it would be time to turn the tables.

And Archie, the fake millionaire and self-proclaimed camp con-artist extraordinaire, did not disappoint.

The very next day at breakfast he waited until she was in line in the cafeteria, then came up behind her and began talking just over her shoulder, slowly and quietly, so she could barely hear his voice over the early-morning clamor of the campers.

"So, Viv—can I call you Viv?"

"Absolutely not. Nobody calls me Viv," she said without turning around.

That technically wasn't true—Margot used to sometimes, and Vivian hadn't ever objected—but she wasn't going to begin to allow this little character to start getting personal. Hanging out with him was a business transaction, pure and simple. She was there to learn, not to make friends. If sixth grade had taught her anything, it was that she was finished with friends.

"Okay, fine, VIVIAN," he said with too much emphasis. "The first and most important thing in this game is your attitude."

"My attitude is fine, thanks," she said with a toss of her hair and an eye-roll. She shuffled up the slow-moving line and craned her neck to try to see what the surly CITs were dishing out this morning. She hoped they had something for breakfast other than eggs. She hated eggs. And now that she knew the big CIT was Archie's friend, she was even more skeptical about what he might dish out.

"I don't mean that kind of attitude," he said, though there was no way he could have seen her roll her eyes. "I mean your attitude toward people you want to work on—marks, we call them, in the business."

Vivian snorted, but Archie ignored her. "The point is," he continued, "you need to be friendly, but not too friendly. You have to act like you have plenty of other stuff going on. And more than anything else, you can't care whether or not they believe you when you lie."

"What?" Vivian said loudly, half turning around, until Archie made a strange noise in his throat and she remembered where she was and turned back. Nobody was paying attention to them anyway— most of the kids were busy watching the front door of the mess hall, where Miss Hiss had reduced a nine-year-old girl to tears for attempting to leave the building carrying a piece of toast.

Vivian took a deep breath and tried to look bored, and peered again down toward where the CITs were dishing out the breakfast. Ugh, it was eggs. Scrambled eggs, probably poured out of a carton that had sat in some barely-above-room-temperature cooler for six months. She'd resigned herself to eating toast for now and just hoped there was something, anything, she liked for lunch. "Hoped" being the most important word in that sentence.

"I mean it," Archie said. "I saw how pushy you were with those cupcakes yesterday. It was too much, over the top."

"I do what it takes to get what I want," Vivian shot back.

"But that's the whole problem," Archie said. "If you act like you're trying to convince them of something, you'll never convince them of anything."

"You sound like my grandmother," she complained. It was true. Ama was always coming out with these little phrases that sounded like something she'd found on a plaque in a tourist-trap gift shop. "A friend to everybody is a friend to nobody," and "one man's disaster is another man's delight."

But he didn't hear her comment, because he'd already disappeared. Even when she glanced around—as casually as possible, of course—she couldn't see where he'd gone. Apparently he fancied himself some kind of Mr. Mysterious type.

Oh well, two could play at that game.

Still, over the next two days, Archie taught Vivian many of the little details of how he operated. His approach was even more complicated and well-thought-out than she expected. Though she wouldn't have admitted that, especially not to him.

"Just remember, I'm in charge," he kept saying.

"Fine, fine, I get it, you're in charge," she said, rolling her eyes the tenth time he reminded her. But that didn't seem to stop him from saying it.

Their first lesson was on "the put up," which was

Archie's fancy way of saying finding the right person to target. Vivian hadn't really thought about that idea all that much—the times she'd run little schemes at school, or around the city, she mainly took opportunities when they came up. Just her and Margot, telling stories and getting people to do stuff for them, mostly for fun. It's not like they had a real system. Well, Vivian didn't. Margot was the one who had been using her all along, a fact she preferred not to dwell on.

But that was one more reason to make sure Archie didn't use her either.

But Archie had read books about con artists and how they operated, or so he said. Vivian didn't even know there were books like that. It wasn't the sort of topic she would have researched in the school library.

He had all sorts of interesting ideas on how to get people to trust you. How to be convincing but not too convincing. How to lie like you were telling the truth. And most important, how to persuade people that doing what you wanted them to do was their own idea, which was the heart of any good con.

And, of course, how to choose a target. Archie fervently believed in choosing a specific person for each particular kind of scam.

"The first rule is, know your mark," he confided in Vivian as they waited for a canoe lesson on the third day of camp. Vivian was already dreading falling into the lake, which was brown and gloppy like old pictures she'd seen of the Hudson River from when her mom was growing up in New York. The depressing puddle of water had some French name, but most of the kids called it Lake Joyless. There was a tiny dirt area they called "the beach," but it was not like any beach Vivian had ever seen. Just a patch of bare ground, next to the edge of the reeds choking the edge of the lake. She wondered how they even held swimming lessons in this place. One mouthful of water looked like it would be enough to send the average suburban kid to the ER with extreme intestinal distress. But at least she wasn't standing there alone, even if her only "friend" right now was, well, Archie.

In the distance she could make out something that looked like an abandoned shopping cart, sticking up, rusted and covered in green goo. She shuddered to think what else was hiding beneath the dark surface of the water. "I thought the first rule was about my attitude?"

"That's not a rule, more like a general guideline."

Vivian gave him a wry smile. "I'm not even going to give you the satisfaction of arguing that point. Fine. I need to know my mark. Whatever that means."

"It means you need to be able to size people up. Figure out who you can pull something over on, and who you can't, and choose wisely. For example, I never con the scholarship kids—they don't have anything I want, for one, and they're usually more suspicious. Besides, they're not the ones who deserve it. I try to pick people who I think will believe what I say without a lot of questions."

Vivian considered this. It did make sense. Honestly, it was basically what she'd been thinking about on the bus, though she hadn't really put it in Archie's specific terms. But yeah, she already had a good idea of how to tell who would listen to her tall tales, and who wouldn't. So that wasn't anything earth-shattering. But she did feel a pang of guilt at his refusing to con the scholarship kids. It hadn't occurred to her that he thought of himself as a Robin Hood type character—only hurting the rich, not the poor. That knowledge made her plan to take him down a little bit more complicated.

But only a little.

"What you really want to find is someone who wants something," he continued. "If you can give them what they want—maybe it's friendship, maybe it's gossip, maybe it's the chance to help someone, or to avoid trouble, anything, really—then you can get them to give you what you want, too. The human mind loves transactions."

Vivian nodded, though she wasn't completely sure she understood.

"And that means listening more than talking. Let them tell you what it will take to get them on your side. And why they deserve whatever they get from you. Find out what makes them tick before you ask them for anything," he said. "And then, only then, you can make your play."

Archie cocked his head in the direction of the lake just as a kid from the eleven-year-old boys' cabin (better known as the Bluegills) attempted to get out of a canoe that looked at least fifty years old, with a scuffed wooden hull and the vague imprint of gold painted letters on the side spelling something unreadable.

The boy almost, but not quite, made it onto the decrepit dock, which was the only point that led in and out of anything resembling open water. But as he tried to edge his way past the other boy in the boat, he tripped over one of the wood crossbars and ended up head over heels right in the lake. The canoeing instructor fished him out while the rest of the Bluegills, Chain Pickerels, Rainbow Smelts, and Walleyes stood around doubled over with laughter.

"This is why you need to follow directions, Julian! Go get changed into dry clothes back at your cabin," the instructor said. "And the rest of you, quiet down!"

The boy, soaking wet and with some sort of disturbingly bright green vegetation attached to his hair and his sopping sneakers, grimaced at the other kids and began to squish his way up the slope that led back to the cabins. Archie stepped away from Vivian and stopped right in the boy's path.

"Hey," he said, smiling.

"What do you want?" the boy asked savagely.

"Nothing," Archie said quickly. "Just that, well, I saw the other kid—the one in the canoe? He pushed you when he was getting out of the boat."

"What?"

"I don't want to cause any trouble," Archie hurried on. "I just thought you should know. Maybe it was an accident and he didn't do it on purpose? But . . . it wasn't your fault. You didn't fall. You were pushed."

Vivian tried not to look like she was staring. She had no idea where Archie was going with this, but at least for now, she was genuinely curious.

The soaked boy glanced back at the kids on the dock, some of them still hiding chuckles behind their hands, then looked at Archie again, this time with a very different expression than before. "Thanks," he said. "Good to know."

"No problem," Archie said, and turned back to Vivian as the boy made his sodden way up the hill toward the cabins. "See? He wanted someone to blame. I gave him that guy over there. Now he feels better about himself, and gets to be angry instead of embarrassed. And he owes me something now, whether he realizes it or not."

Vivian watched the boy's retreating back. There was something about the way his tone had changed once Archie told him he hadn't fallen, that he'd been pushed, that jumped out at her. Maybe Archie was onto something here.

But she didn't have time to think too long about that, because Archie was still talking.

If she was learning anything about Archie, it was that he was always talking.

"The next part of our lesson will be the play . . . and then we have the rope," he continued in a tone that Vivian was finding more and more annoying the longer she was forced to listen to it. "But to learn about those I think we need to make a visit to the camp store. So, we'll continue this tomorrow?"

"Right," Vivian said, still watching the wet boy make his way up the hill into the gloom under the trees. As Archie followed, she thought for a minute how weird it was that they had plans tomorrow. Almost like something you might do with . . . a friend.

But of course, Archie wasn't her friend, not at all. He was a rival.

That night, back at the cabin, Vivian was lost in thought when Sasha-from-the-Bus leaned down from her top bunk. "Are you awake?" she whispered.

"No," Vivian said.

"Ha-ha!" Sasha laughed that self-conscious little laugh Vivian found so irritating. "I know you're joking; your eyes are open! Anyway, I wanted to ask you a question?"

"Um, okay."

"We have to pick partners for the races on Friday?"

Vivian looked up at her, confused.

"It's a Shady Brook tradition! Field Day! Potato sack races? Egg drop?"

Vivian squinted at her. She wasn't any closer to having a clue what Sasha was talking about than she had been before. And she was mystified that anyone could get that enthusiastic about anything at Camp Shady Brook. Most of the kids were already depressed, if not by the bug bites or the startling lack of anything resembling fun activities, then by the food, which only got progressively worse with each passing day.

"You have to know! Everybody's talking about it!" Sasha laughed again, though more naturally this time. "Anyway, I was wondering if you wanted to be my partner? I mean, I'm not the best at sports and stuff?" She sounded briefly worried. "I wish they had an art contest, or something like that! I'm really good at painting! At least I think I am? But anyway, Field Day's on Friday, and it's supposed to be fun!"

A vague memory of Boring Counselor Janet talking about some kind of game day swam into Vivian's memory. Along with something about picking partners for the various dull-as-dirt activities. Vivian had been so caught up in learning her new con-artist skills from Archie she hadn't paid much attention to anything else. But all she said was "I thought you'd want be partners with someone like Lily, from your school."

Sasha let out a breath. "Well, Lily is busy? With other people?"

For a brief moment Vivian felt a little sorry for Sasha. It was true that after the first morning, Lily had seemed more interested in hanging out with everyone else but Sasha. And Sasha seemed like a nice enough girl, after all, even if her friend Lily deserved to be pushed into the lake more than that kid Julian. Lily had a litany of annoying habits, not the least of which was her method of draping the entire toilet in toilet paper before she would even sit down on it, then leaving the whole mess behind for the next person to clean up. Janet had called a cabin meeting about "sanitary habits," but all Lily had done was smirk and act like she had no idea who was the culprit. Vivian hated her with every fiber of her being.

"Well, okay, I guess," Vivian said. And when Sasha didn't say anything, she remembered all the things Archie had said and added, "And thanks for asking me! It'll be fun."

"I know! I can't wait!" Sasha said, and flopped back on her bunk with a giggle, sending the whole contraption into a dangerous series of shakes. Vivian gripped the wood frame of the bunk and hoped it didn't all come crashing onto her head. The bunk beds at Camp Shady Brook were held together— barely—with exposed nails and ragged twine, and they dipped and sagged with even the slightest movement.

As Vivian turned over to go to sleep, she realized that was the first conversation she'd had since arriving at camp with someone who seemed to simply want to be her friend. It was almost as if she'd forgotten what that was like.

ARCHIE

The camp store. Unlike almost every other space at Shady Brook, the store was a modern marvel of glorious excess. And so for their next lesson Archie and Vivian visited it together during midmorning break, or what Miss Hiss liked to call "Required Fun."

The point of Required Fun was that campers had to pick an activity to enjoy, but it couldn't be sitting in their cabin, or talking with friends, or writing letters or reading, even if those were activities that the campers in question would, actually, enjoy.

Instead they had to choose from very specific list of supposedly fun activities that were displayed on a large and waterlogged poster next to the door to the main activity hall. Most of them were things like archery practice or lawn bowling (though the word "lawn" was really wishful thinking at a camp like Shady Brook).

However, fortunately for Archie and Vivian, a visit to the camp store was also one of the options.

The store was in the main camp office building, which also housed Miss Hiss's office and was notable for being the only place in the entire camp that was air-conditioned. That alone made it a favorite destination for many of the campers, who would pop inside to gawk at the many things for sale and get a sweet respite from the muggy heat that seemed to, as far as any of them could tell, emanate from the dank, dirty lake itself.

What some kids might expect from a summer camp store—especially at a place like Camp Shady Brook, where almost nothing looked like it had been built or renovated in at least seventy years—was the exact opposite of this place. In fact, the store was absolutely amazing.

This wasn't some half-hearted display of postcards and key chains, not at all. Instead, it was a two-story atrium of wonder. Sure, there were sweatshirts and T-shirts—but these were available for purchase in almost every size and color you could imagine, including neon green, predistressed blue, and three kinds of tie-dye. The store also had toiletries, of course, for the poor camper who forgot his or her toothbrush, but also

high-end shampoos and even perfume. There were
Frisbees, and pens that lit up when you clicked
on them, and stuffed animals wearing tiny Shady
Brook T-shirts and even ergonomic hypoallergenic
pillows for the discerning camper with thirty-five
dollars to spare.

The only thing you couldn't get was a camera
or any electronic devices. Those were strictly forbidden. Instead, each summer Miss Hiss hired a
photographer to follow the kids around and take a
nicely curated selection of shots that only showed
the best side of Camp Shady Brook. Which campers
and their parents could buy, of course—at a hefty
price. One more of her little scams.

Archie had never considered bringing a camera
to camp. He didn't own one, or a phone. And he had
no idea that Vivian had a nice camera of her own,
wrapped in a sweatshirt and hidden deep under her
bed.

"Check this out!" Vivian said a minute after
they entered the pleasantly cool, well-lit room with
its large, shining windows and tastefully painted
walls, so different from the Rainbow Smelts cabin
or the mess hall it seemed like a completely different camp. She picked up a small box from a
table near the door. "It's a hair clip, but it's also
a screwdriver and a ruler and basically a whole
bunch of tools all in one. Like something for a

spy . . . or even a con artist." She grinned at Archie.

"Please," he said, with a sharp nod of his head toward the back of the store where a bored CIT was manning the cash register. "Do I have to teach you how to do everything? Like even how to be quiet?"

Vivian ignored him. "I love this thing and I must have it," she said, flipping the box over. Her face fell, however, once she saw the sticker on the back. "Twenty dollars? For a hair clip? How is that even legal?"

"Welcome to the Shady Brook camp store," Archie said with a wry smile. It was always a shock, the first time it dawned on an excited camper how the store actually worked.

The store was the whole reason kids were required to bring spending money in the first place, because it was an excellent source of revenue for Miss Hiss. Or at least Archie assumed. Certainly she didn't use any of the money spent at the shop on fixing the ancient dock and falling-down cabins, or hiring counselors who had ever worked with— or possibly even interacted with—children before. "But forget about that. I need to show you something even better."

He led her deep into the shop, past the racks of sweatshirts and beach towels and toys, toward the back, where the candy was kept. Because even with all the T-shirts and gadgets, the real highlight of the store was . . . snacks.

Laid out on small shelves were row upon row of every kind of candy a kid could ever possibly want. Not to mention bags of chips and cookies, and a large cooler that held a mouth-watering array of ice-cold sodas, chocolate milk, and sports drinks.

In theory, campers were only supposed to eat treats in the cafeteria. That's why care-package goodies were locked up in a box in the mess hall that was notorious for (a) never being open when a person might reasonably want to get candy, and (b) attracting an unappetizing large amount of ants.

The camp store was different, however. Unlike cakes and cookies from home, treats bought there seemed to be invisible to the prying eyes of Miss Hiss and her staff. It was a wonderland of junk food, all for the taking.

The only problem was the cost.

"Three dollars for a candy bar? What kind of highway robbery is this?" Vivian asked as she and Archie explored the shelves. "I've been on cruise ships with better prices."

Archie gave a quick glance around to make sure no one was listening. "It's a racket," he said. "They have a strongly motivated captive audience and they're the only game in town. You'd be surprised what some of these kids will pay for a chocolate bar after a week of eating Camp Shady Brook food. Three dollars is nothing."

Vivian gave a short, sarcastic laugh. "I have a hard time imagining you paying anything like that for a piece of candy."

Archie smiled. "Maybe not. But this store is the whole reason why kids are required to bring spending money to Shady Brook. This store, my friend, is the reason why you and I have such amazing opportunities here. Keep that in mind."

"Okay, okay, I get it," Vivian said. "The store is important. But I'm not going to buy anything here, not with these prices, and I suspect someone like you isn't going to spend your hard-earned money here either. So what's the point of coming in? Just to look at all the stuff we're never going to buy?"

"The point is the play," he said. "Watch and learn."

VIVIAN

Archie waved his hand at Vivian in that infuriating way he did when he wanted someone to be quiet. She almost kept talking to spite him, but instead just frowned in his direction and stepped backward into the next row, where she could pretend to examine the immense selection of fashion magazines and gum but still keep an eye on him over the racks. If this was lesson time, she was ready to pay attention. That was the only reason why she was hanging out with him, after all.

Vivian hadn't used her camera yet—she wasn't interested in taking pictures of Camp Shady Brook, and it's not like she had any friends she wanted to memorialize—but the fact that that she had it hidden under her bunk gave her a small sense of satisfaction. Whatever this camp expected of

her, she was determined to give it something different in return. She was tired of being played. It was,
finally, her turn to be the big shot. Whether Archie
realized that or not.

"Hey," Archie said, in the eager voice she'd
already begun to recognize as his usual manner
when he approached potential marks. At first she
didn't know who he was talking to, but then she
realized a pair of boys had walked into the camp
store and were standing near the doorway, looking
around.

They turned at the sound of Archie's voice. Vivian
recognized one of them as a kid from the eleven-
year-old boys' cabin, the Bluegills. It was the boy
who had fallen into the lake the day before, the one
Archie had convinced that he'd been pushed.

"You're Julian, right?" Archie asked too loudly,
and with almost too much forced friendliness. Vivian
wondered what he was playing at this time. But she
figured she didn't have long before she found out.

"Yeah," Julian said, taking a step closer and leaving his friend to examine the T-shirts on a rack by
the door. "And you're Archie Drake, right?"

"You know me? Really?" Archie said. "Wow."

"Everyone knows you."

Archie laughed uncomfortably. "I doubt that.
Anyway. I'm sorry to bug you. I just, I just wanted to
make sure you're okay, you know, after yesterday."

The boy's face darkened. "I got a little wet, okay? Though my sneakers are ruined, they won't dry out for weeks, and they were the only pair I had. But I'm fine. That Mike Cooper, though . . ."

"Is he the guy, who, you know . . ." Archie lowered his voice. "Pushed you?"

"He swears he didn't but I know the truth," Julian said. "I told him to stay away from me if he knows what's good for him." He idly picked up one of the candy bars from a shelf, then dropped it like it was on fire. "Three dollars? Come on! Just my luck, my mom didn't let me bring any food from home and the candy here is three dollars?"

Archie smiled ruefully. "Those prices do seem a little high," he said, as though money was no concern of his, and he was just being polite to the regular folk who viewed three dollars as a price that might give them pause. "I guess I should be happy I brought so many chocolate bars from home."

Julian eyed him. "How many chocolate bars did you bring?"

"A couple of boxes. My father insisted. I honestly won't be able to eat half of them while I'm here, I don't know what he was thinking."

Julian's eyes narrowed. "Any interest in sharing . . . them? Or maybe even selling them? As long as you charged less than three dollars, you know kids would be lining up to get one."

Archie took a deep breath. "Selling my chocolate bars? I don't know about that. I wouldn't even know what to charge. And how would I even approach people—not to mention it's probably against the rules, isn't it?"

Julian lowered his voice. "I could help you out. I mean, you helped me out, right? Give me a box of chocolate bars and I'll sell them for you. You won't have to do anything except take the money."

"Well, I don't know . . . ," Archie said. "Are you sure it's okay?"

"Trust me. It'll be fine. I'll give you a dollar a bar. I can sell them for double that around here."

Archie considered the offer. "I'm not sure it's the best idea, but okay. I mean, we're friends, right?"

Julian smiled widely. "Just stop by my bunk after dinner," he said. He turned around and caught the eye of the boy he came in with. "Come on, let's go, this place is a rip-off," he said, and the pair hurried out together.

Vivian came around the corner of the candy rack and stood next to Archie, pretending to examine the bags of potato chips hanging on hooks on the display in front of her. The store was deserted now, except for the CIT at the counter who was still flipping through a magazine.

"I don't get it," she whispered. "What was the point of all that?"

"The point? He thinks he's going to make a killing selling those candy bars he talked me into letting him have," Archie whispered back. "He's already counting the money in his head."

"And he's right," she said. "Even at two dollars each, he'll sell out in hours. And you'll only make half of that. Those chocolate bars probably cost a dollar each to begin with! I don't get it. What kind of scam is that?"

"Ah, but what you don't know, my dear Viv—"

"I told you not to call me that."

"Sorry, Vivian. First, I didn't pay anything for those candy bars, I got them off another camper last year. Second, what you don't know is that once he sells that first box, he'll come literally begging for more. Which I will, after a lot of convincing, provide—but at a higher price, of course. I only have three more boxes, you see, and I'm pretty sure he's going to want all of them."

"Okay," she said. "So this guy is doing the work for you. I get the appeal of that. But I still don't see why you can't just sell the candy yourself and make all the money. It can't be that hard for a guy like you. Why even bother with a middleman?"

"Ah, but there you go," Archie said. "What you also don't know is that mere moments after my friend Julian back there and I complete our second transaction, those boxes of candy bars are going to be confiscated by a CIT who will threaten to report the whole situation to Miss Hiss. Until we let him keep all the candy bars and all the money Julian has already made, of course."

"Oliver," Vivian said. It wasn't a question. She already knew she was right.

"Yes, our good friend Oliver. Then he'll return the candy bars to me, I'll give him his share of the money and keep the rest, and I'll be able to do the same con again next week. What do they call that? The gift that keeps on giving?"

Vivian shook her head in fake disapproval at his deception, but she was smiling. This was excellent, way better than anything she'd ever imagined. Not only because it was a good con.

It was also one more thing she knew about Archie that she could use against him.

ARCHIE

Over the remaining few days of that first week, Archie took Vivian almost everywhere he could without attracting attention to their budding partnership and shared with her the tools of his trade, allowing her to observe everything: the good, the bad, and the occasionally ugly. The way he acted a little awkward when he spoke to the other kids, so they thought he was just trying to be overly friendly and underestimated him; how he shuffled his feet as though he was embarrassed and refused to answer when people tried to find out if he was, truly, related to the entrepreneur Archie Drake; and more than anything, the way he always carefully constructed his cons so it was next to impossible for him to get in trouble.

Even the chocolate sale had plausible deniability—he was just sharing candy with a friend; he had no idea Julian intended sell the bars to kids all over camp.

That was the key to everything.

Of course, what Vivian couldn't possibly know was that a major part of his plan was to keep close tabs on her for the entire week. The more time she spent with him learning how to be a con artist, the less time she'd have to try out any of his techniques on her own—and potentially get them both in serious hot water. And, no less important, the more opportunities he would have to turn the tables on her for tricking him into teaching her in the first place.

"Just like when you do something for them, then they owe you, another way in is to get them to do something small for you," Archie instructed her as the lessons continued. "Get them to give you something, help you with something. Once you get someone to do something for you, even if it's just a tiny little favor, they are more inclined to do big things. I read all about it online."

Vivian made a face. She had zero interest in learning all the stuff he'd read on the Internet during the school year about new cons; she said it was "too weird."

"Okay, something small," she said. "Like what?"

"Well, like a cookie," he said, stopping a younger boy who was walking back to his table with two cookies on a plate. "Hey, can I have one of those?" Archie asked, good-naturedly.

"Um, okay?" the boy said, looking around a little confused. "But there's a whole tray of them—"

"I know," Archie said with a shy smile. "But the cookies go fast and they'll all be gone when I get up to the front of the line. And you did take two. . . ."

The boy looked chagrined, like maybe he'd broken one of the camp's many rules by taking two cookies.

"Okay, here," he said, and held out the plate.

Archie's smile broadened. "You're the best," he said, grabbing one of the cookies and taking a big bite. "What's your name?"

"Sam," the boy said shyly.

"Well, it's nice to meet you, Sam. I'm Archie Drake." The boy's eyes went wide at the name, and he kept looking at them over his shoulder, even as he wandered toward a table in the back, and Archie turned back to Vivian. The boy almost tripped over another kid's outstretched legs, but caught himself.

"So you think I'm spending all this time and energy hanging out with you so I can learn how to cheat little kids out of cookies? That doesn't seem like much," Vivian said.

"Cookies . . . ," Archie said. "Or, you know, cupcakes." He gave her a meaningful look.

"Right, point taken," she said. "Now it's my turn."

They were standing back-to-back so it didn't look like they were together. All around them kids were picking at their food and talking. Nobody seemed all that interested in today's lunch, which was Camp Shady Brook's famous "beef surprise." The standing joke at camp was that the "surprise" part was that there wasn't actually any beef in it. Few people wanted to know what was actually in it instead, though there were plenty of rumors. But the cookies they served once or twice a week were okay, even if they were dry enough to require a full glass of milk to eat a single one. And some of them were even chocolate chip.

Without another word to Archie, Vivian walked over to a table of ten-year-old girls, better known as the Carp bunk, and plopped herself down in an empty seat. "Hi, everyone," she said in a friendly tone to the younger girls, who openly gaped at her. "Are you guys having a good time at camp?" she continued.

Archie listened carefully from a few feet away, though to the rest of the campers it looked like he was merely examining one of the posters of rules that hung on the walls.

"Yeah, I guess so," one of the girls sitting next to Vivian said. "Though I don't really like the food." She pushed her beef surprise around on her plate with her fork, then picked up what may or may not have been a carrot, examined it, replaced it, dropped her fork, and made a small, unhappy face.

"Yeah, the food is pretty terrible," Vivian said. "Except for the cookies. They're okay." She sighed in a theatrical way that Archie thought was a bit over the top, personally. "Too bad they ran out before I got one."

The group of Carp girls shifted uncomfortably in their seats. Sitting smack in the middle of the table was a plate with at least half a dozen cookies on it—obviously one of the girls had brought a bunch of them to share with her friends. Vivian glanced at the cookies, then pointedly looked away.

"Do you, like, want a cookie?" one of the girls ventured.

"Oh, those are yours!" Vivian said. "I wouldn't want to take your cookies."

"But we have a lot of them. I didn't realize they'd run out so quickly."

"Of course you didn't," Vivian said. She smiled, grabbed a cookie off the plate, and stood up at the same time. "Thanks."

She didn't look at Archie as she walked past him and sauntered out of the mess hall, but she did whisper "Easy as pie" over her shoulder as she left.

He smiled to himself. Everything was definitely working out just the way he intended.

And while he hated to admit it, he was also a

little proud of how well she'd done—how quickly she'd picked up on the ruse and made it her own. He wasn't used to being honest with anyone, except maybe Oliver. And yet, this girl . . . It might be nice to have a worthy adversary for once. Even if his real goal was to eventually crush her.

"Are you really sure this is a good idea?" Oliver whispered later that afternoon as they pretended to ignore each other during free swim. Most of the kids avoided swimming in the lake unless the counselors made them, since the only way to get in and out without wading through endless weeds was from the dock, which had its own hazards, including an endless number of splinters and several protruding rusty nails. Still, sitting around on towels on the dirt patch that passed for beach was one of the few reasonably nice ways to spend free time at Camp Shady Brook. As long as you had enough bug spray. "I think you need to keep this girl on a shorter leash. She could ruin everything."

Archie shushed him and looked over at Vivian, who sat by herself on a towel, looking bored. "Trust me," he said.

"Aren't you always saying never to believe anyone who says that?" Oliver said, but Archie ignored him, and walked toward where Vivian was sitting.

He gave a glance around to make sure none of the other the kids were looking over.

"I don't understand how anyone can swim in this lake voluntarily," she said to him.

He laughed, a real laugh, surprising himself. "I think the point is it's not really voluntary."

"Well maybe we should convince the other kids that someone got a flesh-eating virus or something from swimming in there? We'd be doing them all a favor."

Archie smiled, without meaning to. But then he reminded himself why he was even talking to her.

"So, you're almost ready to graduate," he said out of the side of his mouth, looking out at the lake like he was deep in thought. "The final test is to find a mark of your own."

"Really?" she asked, her eyes showing her skepticism. "You're really going to let me do my own con at your precious Camp Shady Brook?"

"Why not?" he said with a broad smile. "It'll be fun. And it'll prove I know what I'm doing. That I can truly teach my method to anyone. Heck, maybe I'll write a book someday."

"Right," Vivian said. She took a deep breath. "Okay, what do I need to do?"

"Well, you know tomorrow's Field Day, right?"

"Um, yeah," she said. "Some of the kids in my bunk were talking about that."

"And there are prizes for the winners, right?"

"Sure, I guess so. . . ."

"I want you to get one of the prizes."

She made a face. "You want me to, like, win the sack race? How is that a con?"

He laughed. "I don't want you to *win* one of the prizes. I want you to *get* one. That's very, very different. And it's most definitely going to take a con."

VIVIAN

Friday dawned, the last full day of the first week at Camp Shady Brook, and the infamous Field Day.

Rumors had flown all week about the fun prizes campers hoped would be presented to the winners in each category: T-shirts, and not the cheap-looking free ones they all got the first day, but the nice ones that didn't itch. Candy. Gift cards to the camp store and a million other places. The stories about what kids might win grew more over-the-top each time somebody talked about it, as though the campers were trying to convince themselves there had to be some reward at the end of such a dreary week of swimming in muddy Lake Joy-less and unsuccessfully avoiding the camp's killer mosquitoes.

Vivian hadn't been paying a lot of attention to

the preparations, other than half-heartedly agreeing to partner with Sasha in the games. She was too busy absorbing everything she could from Archie.

She begrudgingly admitted he was pretty good at this stuff. And she knew that her window for learning it all might be coming to a close, once he figured out she'd lied about staying only one week. Archie didn't know it yet, but she still had a trick or two up her sleeve. He wasn't the only one who knew how to play this kind of game.

If she had any regrets about ruining all the fun they'd been having together, she wasn't about to admit them now.

The most surprising part of Archie's camp persona revealed itself one day outside the camp store. A small boy, maybe nine years old, was sitting on the steps looking dejected. "What's up?" Archie asked, and the boy's eyes went wide—that was the effect Archie had on the younger kids at Shady Brook, who all viewed him as some sort of celebrity.

"Nothing," the boy said. "It's just . . . well, all my friends are in there getting ice cream and I don't have any money, and then my one friend said I couldn't come with them because of that."

Archie smiled, and then bent over toward the boy. "Tell you what, here's a few dollars," he said, pulling some cash out of his pocket. "You go in there and buy any ice cream you want. Get two ice creams. And tell that 'friend' of yours Archie Drake said to leave him alone."

The boy jumped up, going from almost completely listless to full of energy in a matter of seconds. "Thanks! Wow!" he said, his eyes darting between Archie and the money in his hand. He gave them a huge smile and then ran up the stairs to the camp store two at a time.

"What was THAT all about?" Vivian asked. She was honestly so shocked by the scene, she hadn't been able to say much of anything during the whole interaction.

"Just a scholarship kid who needed a little help," Archie said.

"How did you know?"

"Oh, I can tell," he said, giving an out-of-character self-conscious shrug, and then walking off. She stared after him in wonderment. Sometimes it was hard to tell if he was a hardened criminal or Robin Hood. Maybe he was a little bit of both.

"OMG, it's actually Field Day! I'm so excited!" Sasha said as soon as they woke up from their fitful and bug-infested slumber. Throughout the week Vivian's bunkmates had attempted increasingly desperate measures to keep the mosquitoes from eating them all alive at night, so that now almost every surface—from the windows to the bunks themselves—was draped with various items of clothing and bedding doused in insect repellent in a fruitless attempt to keep the bugs away. "Maybe we'll win one of the prizes! That would be so cool!"

Vivian shook her head at Sasha's enthusiasm and scratched at last night's crop of bites. She couldn't believe she was voluntarily hanging out with someone who actually said the letters "OMG" as an exclamation. But then she remembered she had a job to do, so she rolled out of bed and gave Sasha a weak smile. "Great," she said. "I can't wait."

Field Day, despite its name, wasn't held in an actual field, since Camp Shady Brook didn't have anything that could remotely qualify as one. Instead, it was a series of events held all over the camp, including an egg-in-a-spoon race in the dusty bus parking area; a few swimming and canoe events at the polluted lake; and, most disgustingly to Vivian, a "pie-eating contest" that entailed campers pushing their faces into pie tins filled with whipped cream sprayed out of a can and trying to eat as much as possible in one minute. Just thinking about it made Vivian want to hurl.

"I am not doing that, I'm telling you right now," she informed Sasha as they were guided through the various events by Boring Counselor Janet, who as usual, seemed to have very little information about what was actually going on, and even less enthusiasm. Like the campers, Janet had also spent most of the week fending off a feeding frenzy from the local bugs, and had welts up and down her arms and across her face to prove it. She'd coated the ones on her face with some sort of pink lotion that was flaking off in a distracting way as she talked about the plans for the day.

"I think this is not actually pie?" was Janet's only comment when they visited the setup for the pie-eating contest in the mess hall. "I mean, it doesn't look like pie to me. More like a pile of whipped cream in a pan. I guess I'll have to check." She heaved a sigh as though merely finding out the answers to some questions about the events was more work than she could bear to take on.

"Come on, Vivian, it'll be fun!" Sasha said, continuing her attempts to get Vivian to act remotely excited about any of it. "And you don't have to do the pie-eating contest. There're tons of other things. Don't you want to win one of the prizes? I heard they're giving out iTunes gift cards!"

Vivian was pretty sure they were not giving out gift cards or anything else actually worth winning, but she managed a small smile anyway. Because whatever the prizes were, she really did want one. Not to win one, of course, but to scam one off someone else. If only to prove to Archie she was as good a con artist as he was.

At arts and crafts, before the Field Day events started, Sasha was ebullient as she made friendship bracelets alongside the rest of the Rainbow Smelts. "I'm so glad we're doing this!" she confided in Vivian as her hands moved so fast, weaving embroidery floss in and out, they were almost a blur. Vivian herself had no interest in making bracelets. She'd half-heartedly picked a few colors of floss and tied them together, but spent most of arts and crafts time lost in thought, trying to figure out the best way to con one of the kids out of their prize. If this was Archie's idea of a test, well, she was going to pass with flying colors, whatever it took.

"Me too," Vivian said without enthusiasm. They were sitting at a long table in the arts and crafts cabin. The dingy, unfinished wood walls were decorated with paintings campers had done over the years.

"I wonder why they don't let us use the good paints?" Sasha asked, looking admiringly at the painting nearest their table. It was, unsurprisingly, a picture of Joyless Lake. The lake and trees were pretty much the only things worth painting at Camp Shady Brook. But it was nicely done. The nameless former camper—his or her signature long ago faded in the corner—had painted the lake with the sun setting over it, and it almost looked pleasant, the way you might imagine a camp like Camp

Shady Brook would look if you'd never actually set foot on the premises. "I love painting, but I didn't bring my stuff because I thought they'd have some here! But Amanda"—she nodded in the direction of the arts and crafts counselor, who was trying, with zero success, to get Lily and her friends interested in doing anything other than chatting with each other in the corner—"said there isn't enough for everyone so it's not fair? But I don't get that, because not everyone wants to paint anyway? Oh well, at least I like making these!"

She held up the bracelet she'd woven with breathtaking speed. It was a wide band of purple and gray and black.

"Nice," Vivian said, since she felt like she should say something.

"Do you like it?" Sasha asked. "Well, great, because you can have it!"

Vivian was taken aback. "No, that's okay, I don't need to take your bracelet."

"But I made it for you! It's all your favorite colors, or at least the colors of all your clothes?"

It was true, Vivian did wear a lot of black and purple. *Huh*, she thought. She never imagined anyone at camp was paying that much attention to her and what she liked and didn't like. Even Sasha. Or maybe especially Sasha, since she didn't seem to be doing it for any other reason than to be nice.

"Besides, it's going to take you all summer to finish one at that rate!" Sasha said, pointing at Vivian's own pathetic excuse for a bracelet. She'd been so busy ruminating about her con plans, she'd barely finished one row.

"Well, thanks, I guess," Vivian said. She held out her hand to take the gift, but instead of handing it over, Sasha grabbed her wrist and then deftly tied the finished bracelet on with a few quick knots, then cut the dangling extra strings with a pair of scissors.

"Now you look like a real camper!" Sasha said. "And it just proves that we are friends . . . though don't worry, you don't have to make me one! I can tell you don't like doing it!" She gave Vivian a wide, kind smile.

Vivian examined the bracelet on her wrist and felt an odd sensation. Almost sort of like gratitude. It had been a long time since someone other than her parents had done something nice for her. But she shook that thought away, gave Sasha a quick, perfunctory smile, and stood up. "I need to get back to the cabin to get ready. It's almost time for lunch."

"And then Field Day!" Sasha said happily.

"Right," Vivian replied. "Field Day."

Friendship bracelets aside, she had a job to do.

ARCHIE

Archie had swim lessons that morning, but he spent most of the time doing more internal gloating than actual swimming. He had no interest in sports, except as an opportunity to get some of his cons going, and today he was consumed with the idea that by this time tomorrow, Cupcake Girl was going to be out of his hair for good. His only regret was that he hadn't been able to con her—he'd been too busy teaching her his little tricks. He hated to admit it, but she'd been an eager student, and there was something appealing about being able to show off all the gambits he'd figured out over the years to a willing listener. Oliver was fine and all, but he'd never been a truly worthy apprentice. A friend, and a confidante, sure, but sometimes Archie thought that part of it was more important to Oliver than the cons themselves.

Not that Vivian was all that worthy either. But she was closer than most. One drawback of being such an amazing con artist was that most of the kids never even realized how good he actually was.

Not that he cared what any of them thought.

"Come on, Walleyes, I need your full attention!" Tom, the counselor who taught swimming, was yelling from the side of the dock where he stood with a whistle around his neck and a frustrated expression. The campers approached it with wary distaste. The dock was creaking and old, with loose boards, and exposed nails and splinters ready to snag bare feet the minute you stepped onto it. (Tetanus shots were required to attend Camp Shady Brook, but few campers realized, until swim lesson time, how that was more than just a precaution—it was a flat-out necessity.)

Unfortunately, the dock was the only good way to get into the swimmable part of the lake—the beach, or what passed for one, should have been more accurately described as a marsh, it was so choked with weeds and mud. Wading through the squishy muck was something only a few hardy campers ever attempted, and then usually only once.

Julian, the boy from the camp store, sidled up next to Archie, who had almost forgotten about him in the hectic week of neutralizing Cupcake Girl.

"So, it really stinks what happened with the

candy," Julian said in a strangely formal tone, very different from their previous conversations.

"Um, yeah," Archie said. His mind was on other things.

"But that's okay, because you're going to give me my money back, right?" Julian asked. "I mean, I never got to sell the other boxes of candy at all, and that CIT took the money we made from the first one, so it's only fair."

Archie stared at him. "What are you talking about?"

Julian glanced around to make sure no one was listening. "I paid you for that candy and then I didn't get to sell it, and now I'm out of all my cash. At least you should give me half back. We were in this together!" His voice took on a pleading tone. "I was only selling that candy so you didn't have to!"

Archie shrugged.

"Don't you care at all?" Julian asked. "I mean, you're supposed to be rich, and that was all my spending money, not just for camp, but for the whole summer at home, too. I'm going home tomorrow and I haven't even been able to buy a decent T-shirt."

Archie was surprised at his boldness. Usually the victims of his cons just realized they'd made a mistake and moved on, if they noticed they'd been had at all.

"I, er . . . ," he said, his mind working quickly. The last thing he needed right now was a disgruntled mark going off to complain to one of the counselors, or worse yet, Miss Hiss.

"Of course," he said with smooth confidence. "I wouldn't want you to feel taken advantage of—not at all. I'm terribly sorry all of this happened. Let me just get the money together"—here he gave a vague look, as though the amount of money Julian was asking about was so inconsequential he wasn't sure where he'd put it—"and then I'll give it to you." He smiled broadly at Julian, meanwhile making a mental note to avoid the kid like the plague until he got back on the bus.

But Archie still wondered if he'd been wrong in targeting Julian. Not just because of the complaints. But the fact that the boy was so worried about money, and that he'd only brought one pair of sneakers to camp, the ones that had gotten soaked in the lake—maybe he wasn't one of the rich kids after all. Maybe after everything Archie had said about never targeting scholarship campers, he'd actually made a . . . mistake. But he shook that thought out of his head. He'd make it up somehow. He always shared his wealth a little bit with the other kids who had nothing. Maybe he'd pass out some candy bars this afternoon to make himself feel better. Or even stick to his promise, and send Julian some money—once he made up for all the lost time he'd spent training Cupcake Girl, of course.

Honestly, at this point Archie couldn't wait for the buses to leave tomorrow. Those beautiful yellow buses, taking all of his problems away in a burst of exhaust and parking lot dust. It would be a sight to behold, he was sure of it.

At lunch, Oliver was on the serving line again. He hated working in the mess hall, which made his usual grumpy act all the more convincing. "We have a problem with Julian," Archie whispered as he approached the line. He jerked his head toward the Bluegills table, where Julian was watching him carefully.

"Who?" Oliver asked as he stirred something that was either sauce or soup, it was hard to tell. Either way, it had a disturbingly yellow slick of grease covering the top that no amount of stirring could dispel.

"The kid with the candy bars," Archie whispered impatiently. "The one you took the money from. Don't you remember?"

"Oh, right. I knew that scam was a problem," Oliver said under his breath. "Too risky."

"But do you think he might tell Miss Hiss?" Archie hated feeling worried about something so inconsequential as a discontented mark.

But something about how upset Julian had been rattled him.

Oliver shuddered. Then he added, "Whatcha looking at, bonehead?" loud enough that three kids standing behind Archie in the food line looked up in alarm.

"Nothing, okay?!" Archie shot back. "Just give me my lunch and get off my back."

The boys around him nodded in approval as Oliver dumped some pasta on Archie's plate and then moved on to the next camper, as though they hadn't spoken at all.

Archie eyed his plate with disgust. Pasta surprise. Again. Of course, the "surprise" part of the dish wasn't much of a shock to most of the kids— it was the leftover vegetables from every dinner they'd eaten the whole week. He was pretty sure one piece of deformed broccoli that perched on top of the limp spaghetti on his plate was the same one he'd seen sitting in the hot tray two or three times already.

He took a seat at the far end of the Walleyes table with his unappetizing lunch, and tried to avoid the laser stare Julian was giving him from where he sat with his own cabin. This week was turning out much more complicated than he'd ever expected, but he had to keep his eye on the endgame. All he had to do was let Cupcake Girl run her little Field

Day scam and then she and Julian would both go back on their buses and he could get back to his regular Camp Shady Crook business. The unhappy glares from Julian and his friends made him more uncomfortable than he liked to admit. He hoped he was wrong about his earlier hunch—no doubt Julian was just another rich kid who didn't appreciate what he had, and to Archie, just another mark, whatever he'd said about that money being all his cash for the whole summer. He was probably lying anyway. And even if he wasn't, now wasn't the time to get soft, right?

Archie stirred his pasta around and tried not to think about Julian's unhappy face. After all, he wasn't at Camp Shady Crook to make friends.

VIVIAN

Vivian didn't see Archie during Janet's Field Day tour or at any of her morning activities, and he looked annoyed and preoccupied at lunch. But it wasn't like she actually cared about hanging out with him or anything. She was just trying to keep him from ruining everyone's summer.

She finally caught up with him at the start of the first event out in the parking lot. Kids were milling all over the place in their matching Shady Brook T-shirts, raising so much dust Vivian had to cover her mouth to keep from coughing.

Meanwhile, Miss Hiss hovered over the proceedings with such a forbidding expression it was impossible for even the smallest kids to have anything resembling actual fun.

"So this kind of thing is a perfect con setup," Archie said in an instructional tone as they stood with their backs to each other, bored expressions plastered on their faces. "Lots of kids in exciting and new situations—the games, the prizes—it makes them easier to sway. All you have to do is pick your mark." She could hear the smirk in his voice as he added, "I mean, if you're really ready. I wouldn't blame you if you wanted to back out now. This gig isn't for everyone, you know."

Vivian ignored the dig and whispered, "What about her?" as they watched a group of eight-year-olds try, and fail, to carry eggs across the parking lot on teaspoons. One by one, the kids were taken out by potholes and trash and sent sprawling in the dirt, their eggs smashed and broken. Lagging toward the rear of the group was a small girl with a long brown braid who seemed more interested in making faces at her friends on the sidelines than actually carrying anything. By the end she won by default, since she was the only one left with an intact egg.

"No, no," he said. "She's a Brook Trout. We never swindle the young kids."

"Why not? Because it's not fair?" Vivian snorted. "First the scholarship kids and now this! I never would have pegged you as a soft touch. . . ."

"That's not why," Archie said defensively. "It's because they have to keep their money in the office with Miss Hiss, and we don't want her asking any questions. Plus they are too little and clueless—it's no challenge."

Vivian raised an eyebrow. "Okay, fine," she said, though she was a little surprised to see Archie show a glimmer of what in a normal kid you might call a conscience. "Well, if you are so good at picking marks, why don't you make a suggestion?"

Archie glanced around. "How about that girl in your bunk? The overexcited one?"

"Sasha?" Vivian asked.

"Yeah, her," Archie said. "She already trusts you. It'll be easy to get to her. All you have to do is make sure she wins a prize, then she's ripe for the taking."

Vivian considered this. Sasha was annoying, that was true, but she was also very nice, probably nicer to Vivian than anyone else at camp. Actually, she was nicer than anyone at school, too. Vivian glanced down at the new bracelet on her wrist Sasha had made her just that morning.

Conning Sasha seemed wrong somehow, like going one step too far. Sasha's biggest flaw was that she just wanted to be friends. But of course, Vivian could never say that to Archie.

"Nah, I don't think she's the right person," Vivian said. "I'll pick someone else."

"Oh, are you scared?" Archie said. "Afraid you won't be able to pull it off?"

"Of course not!" Vivian said. "It's just that I don't

think it's a good idea, that's all. You said I get to pick my mark, and I don't want to pick her. Besides, she's supposed to be my partner today. So if she wins, I win. And I thought that wasn't the point?"

Archie shrugged and seemed to accept that answer. Vivian was glad she didn't have to explain why she didn't want to scam someone who actually trusted her the way Sasha did. Someone like Archie could never understand.

Vivian thought again. "How about Lily, she's in my bunk?" she asked. "And she's a real snob. Totally needs to be taken down a notch."

Vivian smiled at the thought of getting one over on smug Lily, aka Little Miss I Went to Paris, who had done nothing but look down her nose at the rest of the girls all week. Especially Sasha. It might be especially fun to wipe that self-satisfied smile off her face. And it made more sense to scam someone who actually deserved it. Isn't that what Archie had been saying all along?

"Whatever you want," Archie said, sounding bored. "It's your con."

Vivian walked away from Archie and toward Lily to look her over. As usual, the tall girl was huddled in conversation with her friends from the Rainbow Smelts cabin and only occasionally watching what the other kids were doing. When she did glance up, the judgment in her eyes was clear. "This is so stupid," Vivian overheard her say as she hovered nearby. "I can't even believe they're making us do this." In response, her friends laughed like she'd said something unbelievably hilarious.

Something about Lily's tone reminded Vivian vividly of Margot, who also liked to stand on the sidelines and make little cracks about the other kids, whether it was during gym, or hanging out on the steps after school. Margot was always so sure that she was too cool for anything. That memory made Vivian want to con Lily even more.

The only competition Lily had agreed to participate in was the three-legged race, which was the last event of the afternoon. And she won easily— she'd handpicked her partner, a girl named Mona who had barely said two words all week but was at least six inches taller than anyone else and liked to do pull-ups on her bunk that made the whole cabin shake. Apparently, as Sasha explained after she and Vivian had come in last—they fell down three times—Mona was a serious athlete at home, and proved it when she practically carried Lily over the finish, at least three yards ahead of all the other kids.

After congratulations on their win, all the teams got their prizes, which were not, as Vivian had guessed, fancy gift cards or anything remotely like that. Instead they were small bags of candy, which, considering the cost of candy at Camp Shady Brook, was actually a pretty high-value item.

But that just made Vivian's con all the easier.

She came up next to Lily as her friends were congratulating her on her win. Mona, who had done most of the actual work during the race, was standing off to the side, ignored.

"Do you really want to eat that?" Vivian whispered to Lily, wrinkling her nose. "I mean, ugh."

Lily whirled to face her. "What do you want?" The other girls dipped their heads to hide their smiles.

Vivian leaned in conspiratorially. "It's just that I saw Miss Hiss taking that candy out of the bin in the mess hall this morning. The one that's always filled with . . . ants."

"Ew, really?" Lily said, looking around in disgust at the other winners who were happily digging into their bags of treats. "That's just so, so gross. But typical for this place, I guess. Just . . . here. Get this away from me. I don't want it." She shoved the bag in Vivian's direction, and turned back to her friends without another word.

Archie was grudgingly satisfied with her performance after Lily had flounced off. Of course, what he didn't know was that Lily wasn't supposed to eat candy because of her braces. But Vivian wasn't going to mention that.

"Not the fanciest gambit, but it worked," he

said under his breath as they stood, pretending to ignore each other, near the back of the pack of kids. "I guess this means you've graduated. Good luck. You'll be the best con artist in New York, starting tomorrow."

Vivian smiled at him, but more to herself.

He really had no clue.

ARCHIE

By the next morning three-quarters of the campers had already packed up their belongings, more than ready to get on the buses that would take them back to their families and air-conditioned houses. The kids who were staying longer watched in envy as their friends shoved damp bathing suits and sweatshirts that stunk of bug spray into bags, eagerly talking about ordering pizza and playing video games as soon as they got home.

Camp Shady Brook didn't inspire lingering.

After most of the Walleyes had dragged their suitcases, duffel bags, sleeping bags, and dirty pillows down to the main hall for breakfast, Archie stayed behind in the cabin, empty and quiet for the first time in a week.

He enjoyed these moments, alone in the bunk,

in between batches of campers. It gave him a little time to evaluate the last week and look forward to the next. What had gone right, what could be improved. Usually new ideas for schemes danced in his head like the visions little kids have the night before Christmas.

This week was a little different, however. The money situation had not been good, not at all, and he hadn't been able to develop any brilliant new cons. Instead he'd spent most of his time, and his attention, training Cupcake Girl. Training her, and keeping her out of trouble. (Which also meant keeping himself out of trouble, as he was too aware.)

The only success he'd had was the candy-bar scam with that kid Julian. It had been an unfortunate mistake to pick a kid who took everything so . . . personally. Archie wasn't used to kids being so angry about his cons, at least not until they got home and realized he wasn't who they thought he was. But he chalked it up to experience. He'd choose better next time.

He'd hoped that a chance to turn the tables on Vivian would appear, but so far she'd been very cagey and unwilling to succumb to any of his attempts to get her to hand over some of her own money.

Still, the sacrifice was worth it. His reputation remained pristine, or it would be once his ill-fated mark Julian left, and today Cupcake Girl would get on one of those buses and leave Camp Shady Brook forever. And he had time to make up the money he'd missed out on. There were still five more weeks left of camp, after all.

Archie allowed himself a deep, satisfied smile before he hoisted himself off his bunk and headed off to breakfast. He wasn't in much of a hurry. The last breakfast was usually the worst of the week, as the cooks and CITs cleaned out the back corners of the fridge and cupboards in preparation for the new campers who would get at least one or two nice meals to write home about before the food took its usual steep downhill turn.

He didn't see Vivian at breakfast. She was probably packing with the other girls who were leaving from the Rainbow Smelts' cabin. The older the girls, the longer it seemed to take them to pack up, though they didn't bring any more things than the boys did. Archie spent the meal nibbling on stale toast and hearing people promise to each other that they'd email or text every day once they were back home. But he just nodded and smiled enigmatically, and begged off when people asked for his address. "I'm not really supposed to give it out," he said apologetically. "You know how it is . . . with my family and all." The boys at his table exchanged knowing glances.

He finally spotted Vivian afterward, as the masses

of campers convened on the dirty lawn in front of the main office building. Luggage was strewn everywhere as counselors tossed things carelessly into the storage sections under the buses. Some of the departing campers hugged their friends, or said their final good-byes. But most of them just stood with hunched shoulders, defeated, coughing in the exhaust from the buses and occasionally scratching one of their many bug bites.

Camp Shady Crook had that effect on people.

Archie came up behind Vivian and clapped her on the shoulder. "Well, there you go," he said, with more genuine enthusiasm than he gave to anything except the most potentially lucrative con, and once in a while, Oliver. "I've taught you everything I know."

That wasn't technically true, but honesty had never been Archie's specialty. He continued, "Now you can head back to New York City and use your skills on all the kids there. Good luck! Safe trip! Have fun!"

He started to walk away, back toward the Wall-eyes' cabin and the rest of his summer, but Vivian stopped him.

"Ah, but that's the thing," she said with a strange grin. "I'm not going back to New York."

Archie stared at her like she'd lost her mind. "The bus leaves in a half hour."

"I'm aware that the bus leaves in a half hour," Vivian said patiently. "I'm just telling you that I'm not going to be on it."

"But . . . but you said you were only staying a week. You said that!"

"Are you acting shocked at the idea I might have . . . lied to you?" Vivian said with a snort. "That's pretty impressive, coming from Archie Drake."

"But you have to!" Archie's voice was getting louder and more strident. He couldn't believe what she was saying. "You need to go home, that was the plan."

"I don't 'have to' go home, and actually, I can't. Because my parents are"—she checked her watch—"already somewhere over the polar ice cap, flying to China right now, and they won't be back for a month." She paused. "So I guess it's your lucky day, Archie. Looks like you've got a brand-new partner. For the whole rest of the summer."

She grabbed his hand and shook it firmly.

All he could do was gape at her in disbelief.

VIVIAN

After the other Rainbow Smelt campers—
except for Lily (who was unfortunately
staying the whole summer just like Vivian and
Sasha-from-the-Bus)—went, well, back on the
bus, Vivian returned to her bunk and gave the
cabin a full once-over. Now was her chance to get
things just the way she wanted. If she was going to
stay here—and she was, if only to see the expression on Archie's face when she stole all his marks
out from under him—she wanted to make sure
she had the best accommodations possible.

This was no easy task in the Rainbow Smelt
cabin. Or in any of the cabins at Camp Shady
Brook. Aside from the five sets of bunk beds there
was just the small bathroom with its even smaller
pair of showers and then, off to one side, Boring
Janet's tiny private room. Since the cabin was

empty for the first time in a week, Vivian poked her head inside Janet's room to look around. The bed was laid out with a floral pink bedspread and pillow shams that a ninety-five-year-old grandmother would consider "a little too much." A large, fluffy stuffed lamb with a pink bow around its neck lay on top of the whole monstrous scene. The entire dresser was covered in ointments and creams, most of them related to the bug bites and poison ivy that seemed to seek out Janet everywhere she turned.

Vivian shuddered and closed the door.

Looking around the main cabin again, she decided that before her new cabinmates joined her later, she would need to choose the best bunk. Bottom bunks were definitely the better choice at Camp Shady Brook. The tops creaked and shook all night, making the girls feel like the whole setup was going to collapse. Obviously, if that happened, being on the bottom would not be great, since the camper sleeping there would be probably be crushed to death. But Vivian reasoned that she'd take that chance if it meant getting a decent night's rest.

She also wanted to be by a window, for the meager breeze that sometimes came off the lake at night. However, she'd learned it was important to choose her window carefully, since not all the screens were intact and the mosquitoes, vicious enough during the day, were absolutely relentless at night, dive-bombing the campers like an invading army.

Finally, she wanted to be close to the door, in case she needed to sneak out. It was always better to be able to make a hasty exit. She figured she'd invite Sasha to bunk with her again. She seemed innocent enough to accept any excuse Vivian might give for her planned escapades, which would be useful if she had to do anything behind the counselors' backs. And Sasha was, Vivian had to admit, nice. Even though Vivian usually thought of being "nice" as a personal flaw.

She knew Archie was furious about her treachery. But that was his problem. Besides, she was only using his own methods. And she knew she had him good. She knew way too much for him to do anything to stop her. And he had something she wanted. No more messing around with cookies and candy; she wanted to really learn how to run cons. The big ones. The real ones. For money.

And that was enough to make her want to hang out with him—at least until she figured out enough of his tricks to beat him at his own game. There were five more weeks of camp, after all.

Unfortunately, the beginning of the new session didn't go nearly as well as she hoped. Vivian knew Archie wasn't going to be pleased with her sticking around, but she hadn't expected the plan he cooked up to use her as his partner in crime.

"Okay, you've got to understand—if we're going to do this, you've got to dress the part," he said not-so-patiently when they met up during rest period. The camp was quiet and deserted, since the new campers wouldn't arrive until the next day.

As for most of the kids who were unlucky enough to stay behind, the grim reality of their situation was slowing sinking in. It wasn't a mood that inspired fun and games.

"But I don't want to wear a camp T-shirt every single day," Vivian grumbled. "And I despise shorts. I only brought some because my mom bought them and made me. I wear jeans. Jeans!" she grumbled. "If you're trying to make me look like some stereo-typical nerd, I swear, you'll be hanging from the flagpole in your underwear before Miss Hiss blows her air horn tomorrow morning. I don't care what kind of so-called criminal mastermind you think you are. This is not what I signed up for."

"You want to be my partner, right? You want to stick around here and learn everything I know?" Archie shot back. "Then you need to do what I say."

"As you keep mentioning," she grumbled.

"And I'm not trying to make you look like a nerd," he said with an irritating amount of calmness. "I'm trying to make you look like a normal, average camper. A nice girl from the suburbs. Someone who would never, ever be a con artist and would definitely never hang out with one."

Vivian grimaced and sighed. It caused her actual physical pain to admit it, but he had a teeny-tiny little bit of a point. Most of the girls at camp dressed like this. Maybe it would actually be easier to brainwash the other campers into thinking she was one of them if she looked more like they did.

"No way I'm wearing Crocs, though," she said with warning in her voice. "I have to draw the line somewhere."

"Fine," he said. "But no boots. Sandals or sneakers, that's it. No more boots."

She let out a long, deep breath. "You're killing me here, you know that?"

He smiled his most infuriating smile. "Hey, you're the one who wanted to be my partner. So you need to do what I say. That's the first rule. And the second rule is: I run the show. You can't do anything on your own. Do you understand?"

She nodded, but she was still frowning. If this was what being Archie's partner was going to be like, the sooner she figured out how to turn the tables on him, the better. She was already imagining the outfits she'd make *him* wear when she was finally the one in charge.

Sasha, at least, seemed to truly appreciate the "new Vivian," if that counted for anything.

"You seem different today?" Sasha said when

they were walking to dinner the next evening along with the rest of the new Rainbow Smelts. "More, like, normal? No offense!"

"Yeah, right, normal," Vivian said with a sigh. Still, if Sasha bought the whole ridiculous "normal camper" disguise, then maybe the rest of the camp would.

ARCHIE

Archie was pretending he was okay with the new arrangement, but inside, he was livid at the prospect of Vivian sticking around. "This is all I need," he muttered to Oliver. "Another five weeks of Cupcake Girl."

"I told you it was a bad idea to get involved with her," Oliver said. "For the record, I told you that the first day of camp."

"Don't strain your arm patting yourself on the back, Oliver," Archie said. He hated when Oliver disagreed with him. It felt like home, where everyone always acted like he was in the way.

Oliver ignored the remark. "And her name is Vivian, by the way. If she's going to be our partner, you should start calling her that."

"Fine," Archie said. "But I was hoping she'd be gone and we could get down to business. And now

I have to come up with a plan that will get her to leave us alone, for good." He'd been so looking forward to seeing the last of her as she stepped onto that bus.

"And she's not that bad, you know," Oliver said suddenly. "I mean, as a person."

Archie stared at him. "Are you going soft?"

"Of course not," Oliver replied. "I'm just sharing my observations. Isn't that what I'm paid to do, Boss?"

Archie ignored Oliver's remark and decidedly snarky tone. The last thing he needed was Oliver, his aide-de-camp, being taken in by someone like Vivian. Besides, it was all Oliver's fault they didn't know she was staying. He was supposed to check up on that kind of stuff, wasn't he? Or what was the point of having a CIT on the payroll?

They were walking in the out-of-bounds woods near the old boathouse to meet up with Cupcake Girl—Vivian—to go over the plans for this week's cons. But all Archie could think about was pushing her into the lake. Especially once he saw her standing there in her stupid camp T-shirt—she'd ditched the pigtails, but she had her hair in the messy sort of ponytail most of the girls at camp seemed to favor—with a very self-satisfied smile on her face. He was beginning to learn that particular smile was never a good sign when it came to Vivian.

"Okay, before we get started I have some bad news," Oliver announced once they'd checked to make sure no other kids were near enough to hear them talking. "Guess who's back this week? I hate to even say it. Mitchell the Unconnable O'Connor."

Archie let out a groan.

"Connable-oh-connor? What kind of name is that?" Vivian wondered.

"Unconnable," Archie said with a dark grimace. "Mitchell O'Connor, better known as Mitchell the Unconnable." He sighed deeply. As if this summer could get any worse.

Archie had met Mitchell for the first time the previous year. Mitchell was a year younger, so he'd be in the Bluegills' cabin this summer. He was a friendly and calm boy, small for his age (though still taller than Archie, a fact he did not like to dwell on) with light brown skin and closely cropped dark hair. Archie had pegged him for a perfect mark the minute they met, but he couldn't have been more wrong. Something about the kid made him completely impervious to any and all cons. And not because he saw through them—or was a tattletale—but because he just didn't seem to respond to anything Archie threw at him. And his inability to be conned was infectious. He could take down a whole expertly designed scam with a simple question, and anyone within earshot would suddenly be listening to Mitchell being all "reasonable" instead of to Archie spinning whatever web he was trying to weave.

Archie hated him.

"And what's the big deal about this kid?" Vivian asked.

Archie heaved another deep sigh. "He can't be conned—not by me, not by you, not by anyone. He just doesn't respond to them at all, I don't know what it is, but I don't like it, and I don't know how to fight it. Trust me, I've tried."

"Hah," Vivian said. "I never thought you'd admit that *anyone* was unconnable."

"It's not something I'm happy about, but let's face it, the biggest part of knowing your mark is knowing who isn't one," Archie said with a rueful shake of his head. "Anyway, he's back, so we'll just stay away from him."

"As far away as possible," Oliver said, and grunted.

Vivian nodded, but she was still smiling in that way Archie was learning to despise.

VIVIAN

Archie's first scam for this week was a ruse he called "the Flop."

The supplies were pretty basic. He'd taken one of the candy bars he'd acquired last year, stepped on it, tore the wrapper a little bit, and covered it with glue and dirt. He called it his "Tricks Bar."

"Get it?" he said to Vivian, snickering.

"Yes, I get it, it's just not actually funny," she said.

"It's a little bit funny," he said.

"It's not."

Archie made a face at her.

To make the con work all they had to do was convince someone who bumped into Vivian—now dressed as a naive, somewhat clueless "normal, average camper"—that it was their fault the candy bar was ruined.

"It's a classic con, one of the greats," Archie said. "This is the basis for millions of dollars of insurance fraud."

"Fantastic," Vivian said. She took the dirty prop gingerly in her fingers, and examined it with distaste. It was hard to imagine a dirty candy bar could be that successful at conning people. Still, if this was a truly classic con, it was the kind of thing she was hoping to learn, after all.

Later that day, she put it to the test.

"Oh gosh, I spent the last of my money on this," Vivian moaned, after she was bowled over by one of this week's new Walleyes who was playing Frisbee by the lake during Required Fun. "And now look at it! It's completely covered in dirt."

"I'm really sorry," the kid said. He was big, much bigger than Vivian, but he did look truly apologetic. "I didn't mean to knock you over. Really! It was an accident."

Vivian stared at the disgusting candy bar, with its torn wrapper and dirty coating. She blew on it, to get some of the dirt off, but it didn't help. Then she put one hand to her head. "Maybe I need to go see the nurse. I think I might have hit my head on a tree root when I fell down."

She'd actually fallen very carefully and painlessly, thanks to Archie's instructions. But of course the boy didn't know that.

And now, instead of just looking sorry, the boy also looked alarmed. "No, you have to be okay! I mean, we're not really supposed to be playing Frisbee over here but the Northern Pike are using the grass on the other side of the building so . . ."

Vivian just gave him a forlorn look and her lower lip trembled like she was going to cry.

"Oh God, please don't be so upset, I'm really sorry," the boy insisted. "You know what?" he added, reaching into his pocket and pulling out a five-dollar bill. "Here, take this. You can buy another candy bar. Two candy bars, maybe!"

Vivian smiled at him, her eyes shining. "Really? I mean, I don't want to take your money!"

"No, take it," the boy said decisively. "Get another candy bar. Just do me a favor, and don't tell them we were playing Frisbee over here, okay? Promise me?"

"Of course," she said sweetly, and pocketed the bill. It was surprisingly easy, just like Archie had said. And for now, at least, she decided, she didn't feel bad about doing it. As Archie always said, these kids had it coming to them, right? That was the whole point of these cons, giving kids what they deserved. And sure, some of the kids seemed nice, but Vivian knew better than to trust that sentiment. Any reservations she had about taking things, she pushed to the back of her mind. For once, she was the one with the power. Or she would be, once she figured out how to get rid of Archie. It didn't matter that doing this stuff was kind of, well, fun? But she'd been down that path with Margot. Pretending to be someone she wasn't was way easier than being herself and having that turn out to be horrible. Archie was too much like Margot for her taste, anyway. That alone was reason enough to defeat him.

All that week Vivian kept a smile on her face and acted like she loved the cons, but inside she was chafing under Archie's direction. Who did he think he was? Sure, he knew a lot about cons, but he wasn't the only person who had ever scammed anyone. He wasn't the world's greatest expert or anything. He was just a stupid kid who thought he was smarter than everyone else and had a chip on his shoulder because he was poor. There had to be a way around that. There had to be.

Her only solace, as much as she hated to admit it, was hanging out with Sasha-from-the-Bus.

"Let's see if we can get Amanda to let us paint today!" Sasha said as they walked to arts and crafts. She seemed so much more confident this week, walking close enough to Vivian they could have hooked arms (though even Sasha knew better than to try that). "I think if I could just get my hands on some decent paints, I could paint a beautiful picture of the lake—maybe at sunset, when you don't see all the weeds and those weird metal things that stick up in the middle?"

Vivian nodded, half listening. Up ahead, Lily was walking with her new friend, a girl named Patrice who'd just come to Camp Shady Brook this week. Already Vivian could tell Lily had a "type"—her friends all seemed to have the same smooth, light hair, and interchangeable smug expressions.

As they approached the arts and crafts cabin, Vivian noticed a boy standing with some other kids from the Bluegills' cabin. She realized, with a start, it was Mitchell. Mitchell the Unconnable, the kid Oliver had pointed out at dinner the previous night, the only camper Archie had never been able to con. She glanced at him curiously as they went past. He looked normal enough. A little on the short side, but he was probably only ten or so. He was talking and laughing with his friends, like any other kid. She wondered, briefly, what it was that made him such a difficult mark. Was he really smart? Was he a con artist himself? She had no idea. But there had to be something that made him so special that even Archie wouldn't approach him.

And maybe, she thought, Mitchell the Unconnable was the key to finally taking down the Great Archie Drake.

Her reverie was interrupted by Sasha, who was still talking.

"So anyway, what's your school like? Mine's just kind of small and boring!" She laughed.

"My school?" Vivian asked.

"You do go to school, right? In New York? That must be really exciting! Your friends must be so cool!"

Vivian let out a short laugh. She definitely didn't want to explain to Sasha, of all people, that she didn't have any friends at school. She'd burned too many bridges. By the end of the year, nobody would even look her in the eye, because they were afraid she was just like Margot, even though Margot wasn't her friend by that point either. If she'd ever been. So all Vivian said was, "Yeah, they're cool." And then, to change the subject, she added, "Let's go see if we can get Amanda to finally give us those paints."

ARCHIE

Already the second week of camp was turning out to be as much of a disaster as the first. The news that Mitchell the Unconnable was back was only one of the many reasons why Archie was beginning to think this was going to be the worst summer at Camp Shady Crook ever.

His biggest source of worry was, of course, Vivian. Because try as he might, he couldn't get her to give up on being his partner, no matter what he did.

His first idea was to pick an outfit she would hate so much that she would rebel against working with him. Maybe she'd even try to get sent home. But, as much as she complained about the silly "normal camper costume," once they started conning people with the new disguise, she seemed right in her element. They made fifteen dollars, just from that stupid candy bar, and by dinner she was almost cackling with how easy it had all been.

Which just made his job that much harder.

The next day he tried a new approach. "I've got a great idea for us to pull off," he enthused during one of their secret meetings around the far side of Joyless Lake. They always kept a healthy distance from the old boathouse, since everyone knew it housed at least six nests of angry bees, but it was one of the few private places they could talk. "The only hard part is you need to get hit in the head with an oar."

"What?"

"Not hard, or anything. Just a little tap."

"I am not letting you hit me in the head with an oar!" she announced, loud enough that he gave her a pointed look and shook his head toward a group of campers canoeing not far from where they stood. No one was supposed to notice them talking. Not if they wanted to keep up the pretense of not being friends.

"Not me, someone else. Maybe that Peter kid from my bunk? He doesn't look very strong."

"This is a ridiculous conversation. I don't even want to know *why* you think I should get hit in the head with an oar, because it's not happening."

Archie frowned. "But we could make a lot of money. . . ."

"Why don't *you* get hit with an oar, then? And I'll do whatever you were going to do?"

"That would never work," he said, and pursed his lips. "What if it was someone from the Smallmouth Bass cabin that hit you? They're all, like, nine years old. They can barely lift an oar, much less hurt anyone with one."

"THINK OF SOMETHING ELSE, ARCHIE. NO OARS. AND ABSOLUTELY NO HEAD INJURIES." She was yelling now, not caring that the kids in the distance might hear them.

"Well, what, then? You're the one who wants me to tell you how to swindle people." He paused. "Honestly, I just don't get it."

"Get what?"

"Any of it," Archie said. "You live in Manhattan. Your parents sound, well, rich. At least to me. Why do you even care about getting five dollars from some random kid? Why does it even matter? You could just ask your parents for five dollars, I bet."

"It's not about the money," Vivian said. "And you don't know anything about me or my family—" She stopped for a moment, like she was almost going to say something else, but she just said. "Forget it."

"Come on, if we're going to work together, I really want to know."

"I'm sure you do," she said, with more force than

he expected. "You're just like everyone else, looking for an in, a way to get to me."

For once Archie didn't have anything to say.

"Here's the thing," Vivian said. "If I've learned anything, it's that most people are terrible. You're terrible. Oliver's terrible. Miss Hiss is terrible. Did you know today I heard her refusing to give one of the little Brook Trouts a Band-Aid because they, and I quote, 'don't grow on trees?' Face it, Archie, most people are just out for themselves. And if you give them the opportunity, then they'll take you for a ride. If someone wants to take advantage of me, well, I'm going to get there first."

"So you don't trust people at all?"

She laughed. "Should I? Should I trust you? I see what happens when people trust you. You may be better at this kind of game, but everybody is playing it. Even if they say they're not."

Archie had never thought of it that way. He'd always seen his targets as wealthy innocents, ripe for the picking, but not as rivals playing their own games. He was Robin Hood, taking money from the rich and giving it to the poor—well, at least him and Oliver. And some of the scholarship kids. Even if sometimes he messed up a little bit. Like that kid Julian, from last week. He didn't like to think about that. He made a mental note to send Julian some of the money he'd earned so far this summer.

"But what makes you so sure you're right?"

"I just know I'm right, trust me." She laughed again. "Trust me, trust me, trust me. What a con artist should never say. That's rule forty-two or something, right?"

Archie just shook his head. Already this girl was proving to be smarter than he'd ever expected. And, he hated to admit, more like him than he'd ever realized.

Which only made it even more important to eliminate her—or at least get her to lose interest in scams altogether. But he still had one more trick up his sleeve. And then he could maybe get rid of Cupcake Girl for good.

Once the second week was over and the hopeless cases, aka new campers, had turned up and taken their places in the dingy bunks, Archie met up with Vivian and Oliver under the trees near the lake to go over that week's successes and failures.

"This was a great week, wasn't it?" Vivian was gushing. "We made tons of money. I have to admit, that Flop scam really worked. Even with the stupid outfit."

"We did pretty well," Archie said with a smile. "Though I did a bit better last summer, I have to say. Fewer . . . distractions."

"Okay," Vivian said, looking at him warily. "Enough

with the small talk. I know we made a lot of money this week. So where's my cut?"

"Cut?" Archie said, the picture of innocence.

"My cut, my share!" Vivian snapped. "I worked all week on your little scam! I had kids knocking me into the dirt three times a day. I should get some of the money. You can't tell me you're going to take it all!"

"I'm not taking it all," Archie said.

"Really?"

"I'm giving some to Oliver, of course."

Oliver allowed himself a small smile but said nothing.

Vivian's voice got louder. "So Oliver gets paid and I don't?"

"Oliver does a lot more than you know," Archie said brightly. "Trust me, I keep careful records."

"Oliver serves mystery meat and pushes third graders into the lake when they don't walk fast enough to swim lessons," Vivian shot back. "I'm the one who has been working day in and day out, making money. For *all* of us."

"Well, that was the deal. You wanted to be my partner and learn, and so I've been teaching you," Archie said. "Nobody ever said anything about you getting paid. If you don't like it, why don't you get yourself kicked out and go home? That's what you were hoping to do from the beginning, right?"

"How do you know that?"

"I have my sources." He didn't really know what she'd been planning—he was just guessing, but from the expression on her face, he suspected he'd guessed right.

"Well, I can't go home. My parents are in China. Like it or not, you're stuck with me. So hand over my share of the cash."

"No," he said, his eyes defiant. He knew how unhappy she'd be once he refused to share the bounty with her. But would she be unhappy enough to walk off and quit? That's what he was hoping.

"Well, then—"

"Then what?" he interjected. "You'll tell on us? That'll mean telling Miss Hiss everything you've been doing the past two weeks. You'll be sent home in five seconds. I'm sure your parents will be so pleased when they find out they have to come all the way back from China just because you got kicked out of camp."

He watched as Vivian gritted her teeth. "That's it," she said, her voice shaking with barely contained rage. "I'm not doing this anymore."

"Not doing what anymore?"

"Not being your little performing monkey! For no money! This is not what I signed up for, Archie Drake!"

Archie gave her a placid smile. "Well, fine, if

that's what you want. But you know the bargain. You either work with me or you don't work at all. So no more cons for the rest of the summer."

"Are you kidding me? I never agreed to that." She paced back and forth. "I can do whatever I want. You can't stop me."

"Come on, Vivian!" Archie said, a crack showing in his usual calm demeanor. "In four weeks you'll have all of New York City at your feet, all thanks to me and what I've taught you. All I'm asking is you leave Camp Shady Crook to me! This place isn't big enough for two con artists. You know that."

"Nope," she said, and gave him that smug smile he hated with the fire of thousand suns. He could tell there was no way she was giving up now.

Archie's mind veered wildly. Obviously his secret plot hadn't worked. He'd tried to humiliate her, tried to get her to give up. But he'd underestimated her. A mistake he wouldn't make again, he was sure of it.

He frowned, and finally spoke. "How about this— how about a little . . . bet."

She cocked her head to one side. "What kind of bet?"

"A con bet, of course. It's simple. The first person to get the money wins."

"Wins what?"

"Camp Shady Crook, of course," he said. "And all the opportunities that come with it."

"Okay . . . fine. I'll take the bet. Only because I know I'm going to win," she said. Finally, an opportunity to really take over from Archie, and show she was worth being in charge, even if it was just of a stupid summer camp. "So, who's the mark, mastermind?"

Archie thought again, and a slow smile spread across his face. "How about—Sasha?"

VIVIAN

She'd put up with so much this week—the stupid outfit, the crazy schemes. But it was all because she was expecting a payout, some sort of confirmation of all her hard work. Instead she'd lied to people, dressed like a dork, and fallen on her backside so many times, she was convinced she'd have a bruise on her tailbone for years to come. And for what? She was still at Camp Shady Crook, still friendless, and she had nothing to show for it. And now this.

"You want to con Sasha-from-the-Bus?"

"No, I want *you* to con her. Or try to."

"That's stupid. That would be way too easy."

"Oh, would it?" He gave her a strange look. "If it's so easy, then why don't you want to do it?"

"I didn't say I didn't want to do it," she said. But inside, she really didn't. It wasn't that she actually liked Sasha; she was annoying and peppy and always trying to be involved in whatever was going on—she wore her need for friends like a T-shirt that said, well, I NEED FRIENDS. Probably with a lot of exclamation points. Still, Sasha wasn't a bad person, not really. And the point of conning was to get one over on bad people, wasn't it? Not nice people. Not people who made friendship bracelets and asked Vivian questions about herself and seemed to actually listen to the answers.

"If you don't want to con her, then I will," he said.

"*No*," Vivian said, with more emphasis than she intended. "I'll do it." The gears in her mind were whirring, trying to figure out a way to con Sasha without actually hurting her—something that would seem like a con, but wouldn't make Sasha, well, hate her.

But whatever Vivian could do was probably better than what Archie would come up with. That would be even worse. He could really hurt Sasha. And she couldn't let that happen. "But you can't con her too, that won't be fair," she said quickly. "You have to pick someone else."

Archie laughed. "Great. I can con anyone I want at this camp."

Vivian raised an eyebrow. "Anyone? Even . . . Mitchell the Unnconnable?"

"Well, that's different," Archie said, taken aback. "He's a special case."

"Scared?" Vivian said. "Afraid you can't pull it off?"

"Not any more scared than you are," Archie shot back.

Vivian gave him an evil smile. "Then fine, I'll con Sasha, but you have to con Mitchell. The first one to get the money—and prove that they got it from the mark, no messing around—wins the whole camp for the rest of the summer. All we have to do is decide how much."

"How about fifty dollars?" Archie shot back.

"Fifty dollars?!" Vivian's voice was loud enough that Oliver looked alarmed. She lowered her voice again. "That's insane. That's a whole summer's worth of spending money."

"But isn't that the point? It's a bet. It's not supposed to be easy."

She sighed. Conning Sasha was going to be hard enough. Conning her out of fifty dollars seemed impossible. Still, she was in too deep to back out now. And from the look on Archie's face, she knew this was the only way she could come out on top, once and for all. "And when I win, you'll leave me alone to do whatever I want?"

"Yes," he said.

"And you won't run any more scams at Shady Brook? You've been the king too long around here, Archie Drake. It's time for a change."

Archie paused. Vivian suspected he was sure he had this thing in the bag, but even he had to take a moment to consider what he was really putting at risk. He was too smart not to. "Okay, fine," he finally said. "But when I win, you'll never con another person at Shady Brook, not only this summer, but ever again."

She paused too, but then she said, "Deal."

And they shook hands.

Vivian's mind was already working out how she was going to win. Because if there was anything she knew, she definitely had to win. This was the moment she'd been waiting for all along. The final power play.

If only to see Archie's face when he admitted defeat.

ARCHIE

That night, the first night with the new Week Three campers, was the bonfire and sing-along. The counselors would perform some silly skits and teach the campers a few useless songs, and everybody would roast marshmallows and eat s'mores.

Just like at any other camp.

This was a calculated move by Miss Hiss, since Sunday was letter-writing day. Thanks to the bonfire, the letters home would be filled with tales of songs and fun, and the parents would rest easy thinking their children were having the time of their lives at Camp Shady Brook. Miss Hiss knew most kids would be home before they had a chance to write another letter, and so the stories about the backed-up toilets and swarms of mosquitoes and the polluted lake would have to wait until their parents' payments had long since cleared. She always made a point of putting on a good face for the new parents. Camp Shady Brook wasn't the sort of place you'd send your kid again unless you had no other choice.

Archie sat toward the back of the crowd huddled around the bonfire, where there were more mosquitoes but less sparks and smoke. He tried to ignore the screeches of a hundred children screaming the words to "Little Bunny Foo Foo" and concentrate on observing Mitchell, the kid who couldn't be conned, undetected.

Mitchell was sitting near, but not exactly with, a bunch of the boys from the Bluegill cabin. He was half listening to the songs, but also, when no one was looking, paging through a large book, using a small flashlight he held cupped in his hand to read the words. He seemed distracted and disengaged from the crowd, something Archie knew was always a good sign in a potential mark.

It was a golden opportunity to figure out how to con the famous Unconnable O'Connor, if he was going to take back his beloved Camp Shady Crook from that interloper Vivian.

It was now or never.

"Hey, Mitchell," Archie said in his friendliest voice as he came up behind the boy, then plopped down next to him in the brown and uneven grass. "Nice to see you back."

"Archie!" Mitchell said. "You're back this summer too! That's great. My cabin is all filled with newbies. I had to miss the first week of camp for my grandparents' anniversary party, but at least I'm staying for the rest of the session."

Mitchell seemed genuinely pleased to see him, a fact that only filled Archie with more disgust. Did this boy not realize he was dealing with a master criminal, not just another camper? What was his deal? Why was he always so . . . nice? It was infuriating. And perplexing. Archie wasn't used to people being nice to him for anything other than their own gain. At home he'd learned the hard way—a smile too often ended in a punch, or at minimum, handing over his lunch money.

"Whatcha got there?" Archie said, pointing at the book.

Mitchell gave a self-conscious laugh. "It's a book," he said. "Well, obviously it's a book, ha-ha."

"You brought a book to a campfire sing-along?"

Mitchell shrugged. "I'm not that into the singing," he said. "But the fire is pretty cool."

Archie nodded. His mind was working furiously to find a way, any way, into the connable part of Mitchell's brain. It had to be there. Everybody had an angle, something for Archie to exploit, even the Unconnable O'Connor. But the most important thing was to keep the conversation going while he found an in. "What's so great about this book?"

Mitchell looked up again. "Oh! It's about pirates. I'm kind of into pirates. Real ones, not the kind you see in movies—and this book"—he held it out and in the dim light of the flashlight Archie could see a large picture of a ship flying the Jolly Roger— "explains all about them."

"Oh, neat," Archie said. He didn't know—or care—much about pirates. He liked reading about criminals, of course, but devious ones, not the kind that fired cannons and burned boats hundreds of years ago. But he could tell that Mitchell was really into the topic, so he plowed on. Faking an interest was one of his pet strategies. "So, what have you learned?"

Mitchell seemed pleased at the question, and closed the book, leaving a finger inside to mark his place. "All sorts of stuff. Like, most people think pirates only worked on the sea, but there were river pirates, too. Smaller groups that attacked ships on rivers—even here in the United States."

"Wow," Archie said. He wasn't pretending this time—he honestly never knew that before. "And did they bury treasure, too?"

"Well, not all pirates buried their treasure. Most of them spent it," Mitchell said. "It's mainly movies that talk about stuff like that. But there is a legend about a buried treasure along the Connecticut River, in Massachusetts—people say that Captain Kidd actually traveled the river to find a place to bury his treasure. And he left it on an island—" Mitchell open the book and flipped to a new page, checked something, and then said, "Clark's Island, they call it. But no one was ever able to claim it."

Archie nodded. An idea was taking shape in his head. "That's pretty neat," he said. "That means there could be treasure literally anywhere."

"Well, not anywhere," Mitchell said with a smile. "Most places have been dug up for buildings and roads and stuff, and anything buried would have been found long ago. It would have to be someplace remote. Out of the way, you know."

"Interesting," Archie said. He stood up slowly and brushed the dirt off his shorts. "Very interesting."

When he wandered back to the Walleyes, his mind was a maze of new ideas. Not about pirates, exactly, but about a new con. One that might just work on even Mitchell the Unconnable.

The loudly singing campers had moved on to "Do Your Ears Hang Low," when Oliver threw himself down on the grass next to Archie. "Make it stop, for the love of all that is holy, make it stop."

"You're not supposed to talk to me in front of the other kids," Archie said from the side of his mouth, without looking at Oliver.

"Oh, come off it for a minute, for once. Nobody

cares, it's dark, and I've had a bad day. One of the Longnose Gar puked on my bed."

Archie laughed. He couldn't help himself. For reasons clear to no one who knew him, Oliver was always assigned to be the CIT for the smallest boys in the camp. And even more mystifying, they adored him—followed him everywhere, like a pack of small, awkward puppy dogs in matching Shady Brook T-shirts and untied sneakers.

"It's not funny, Drake! These kids are a nightmare. They've been here half a day and one of them already threw up, another one got a bloody nose, and two of them wet their pants. I doubt half the cabin will survive the week."

Archie laughed again. "Well, if it makes you feel any better, I think I might have a plan to win our bet, con Mitchell, and get that little cupcake thief off our backs for good."

"Really?" Oliver sounded uncharacteristically concerned. "I mean, are you sure this bet is really a good idea? Mitchell's okay enough, and Sasha's actually really nice. I don't mind conning some of the knuckleheads, but why do we have to con the good kids? That doesn't make sense at all. Even if it makes Vivian back off. Which, by the way, I'm not one hundred percent convinced is necessary."

"It's not about Mitchell and Sasha, it's about neutralizing Cupcake Girl," Archie said impatiently. He hated when Oliver acted all "reasonable" about things. It made his job as a criminal mastermind all that much harder. "There's always collateral damage, but you have to think about the big picture. We've already wasted two weeks of camp."

"But why do we have to beat her at all? Why can't you just give her a cut like she asked?" Oliver asked. "She's not too shabby at these cons herself, you know. And isn't it more fun when we all do it together? It makes it feel more like a game."

"Who said this is supposed to be fun?"

Oliver shrugged. "Okay, fine, you don't like her, I get it. But what if she wins? Have you thought about that?"

"There is no way she's going to win!" Archie was incredulous. "You do realize who you're dealing with, don't you?"

"I know, I know," Oliver said. "Just don't get too cocky, and be careful."

"When have I ever gotten too cocky?"

Oliver didn't answer.

"Anyway," Archie said slowly, thinking. "If my idea is going to work, I'm going to need to get to a computer."

Oliver sighed. "Really? Again?"

"Look, I know it didn't work out last year, but this time, it has to. It's important."

"But that means sneaking into the office." Oliver

frowned. "And we came so close to getting caught last year. I still have nightmares about Miss Hiss chasing us into the woods. I have no idea how she didn't figure out it was us."

"I know, but this time we'll be more careful." Archie's voice took on a conniving tone. "I know it's not going to be easy. But I'm not asking you to do anything but be my lookout. There's no way you can get in trouble. All you have to do is say one of the Longnose Gar is sick and you were looking for Miss Hiss, or the nurse. Do you remember the signal?"

"Of course I remember the signal. Do you think I'm an idiot?" Oliver said, rolling his eyes—an unusual gesture for him. He put his hands around his mouth and called out, "Caw, caw."

"Not here!" Archie hissed. "Save it for Wednesday night. After Parents' Day. That's always the best time to fly under the radar around here."

The campers had moved on to "There's a Hole in the Bucket," and now Oliver looked like he was going to throw up just like the poor little Longnose Gar. "I can't take much more of this," he said, standing up. "If you want to try to con that Mitchell kid, fine, I'll help you, even if it's probably a lost cause. But for now I've got to make sure one of those snot-nosed little kids hasn't fallen in the lake."

VIVIAN

Vivian took the long route back to the Rainbow Smelts' cabin after the bonfire so she could brainstorm. Conning someone like Sasha out of fifty dollars was going to be hard. Not impossible, but not as easy as getting a few dollars or some candy from one of the Bluegills, or even train fare from a grown-up in Grand Central Station back home in New York. This kind of scam would take real planning, and real work.

What was the first rule of con artists? Know your mark. Even though she hated that she could hear Archie's instructions echoing in her head, she knew he was right. And if there was any mark she knew well at Camp Shady Crook, it was Sasha-from-the-Bus, who'd been hanging around her since the first day of camp. The only problem was that as much as she tried, she couldn't help but like Sasha.

And that made conning her all the harder.

But maybe she could find a way to con her without actually conning her? Just enough to get Archie to admit she'd won, but nothing that would make Sasha mad at her. Something she could easily fix, once the bet was over. And then she'd beat Archie but also not make Sasha mad . . . and she'd win the bet and keep her friend at the same time.

She smiled to herself in the gathering darkness.

It would be easy enough to get Sasha to take the bait. She'd been waiting since the first day of camp for Vivian to notice her overtures of friendship, and once Vivian gave more than begrudging attention, Sasha would be an instant convert to anything and everything Vivian wanted to do. All she had to figure out was what Sasha wanted—and that was easy enough. Because after spending two weeks listening to Sasha's grumbling, she knew the answer: Sasha wanted paints.

It was all she talked about at arts and crafts— how they weren't allowed to use the good materials, just string and beads and construction paper, like the little kids. "I asked my parents if they would send me my watercolors but they are afraid I'd lose them here?" she'd said the other day, with a small sigh. "I'm really disappointed! I thought I'd get to paint nature all summer!"

She'd even checked out the camp store, but they

didn't have anything she wanted, just "like, a bil-
lion colored pencils and Femo clay! I don't want to
sculpt, I want to paint pictures! And I know they
have to have paints because there's all those paintings in the art cabin? I don't know why Amanda
won't let us use them? I asked her and she said we'd
just make a mess, even though I promised I would
be careful!" She let out a very un-Sasha-like sigh.
"I don't see why some kids have to ruin stuff for
everyone!"

"So," Vivian said quietly as they walked toward
the lake for swim lessons the next morning. "I might
have a solution to your paint problem."

Sasha cocked her head. "What do you mean?"

Vivian took a deep breath. "There's this girl—she
doesn't want me to tell you who she is—but she has
a full set of watercolor paints she brought from
home. And she wants to sell them."

"Sell them?"

"Yeah," Vivian said. "She's already spent all her
money and she wants to be able to get more stuff at
the camp store. But she's not really supposed to sell
her stuff, you know."

Sasha was skeptical. "Well, that doesn't sound
right? She's going to get in trouble with her parents
when they find out!"

"That's her problem," Vivian said. "You want the

paints, right? And you'll be able to use them to make wonderful paintings all summer, just like you wanted. I bet you could paint a beautiful picture of the lake, better than anyone else, if you just had the right materials. . . ."

Sasha sighed again. "I do really want to paint the lake? Like, at sunset? Okay, okay! I'll take them! It's not like I'm going to use that money for anything else, anyway?"

Vivian smiled, though internally she was fretting. She hoped Sasha wouldn't figure out what was going on and be mad. But she knew if she could get her hands on some paints from the arts and crafts cabin, then she could sell them to Sasha, telling her they came from that mysterious, unknown paint-selling girl. Sasha would be happy. And then Vivian would take the fifty dollars and show it to Archie, and she'd win. And then the whole thing would be finished.

Of course, getting paints for Sasha meant breaking into the arts and crafts cabin and taking something, and while she'd conned people before, she'd never actually . . . stolen something.

But once she'd won the bet, she'd tell Sasha everything. Heck, Sasha would probably think it was funny, and they'd both have a good laugh at Archie's expense. And then Vivian would give the money back and put the paints back where she'd gotten them, and it would all go back to the way it was before. So it wouldn't even really be a real con. Or even stealing—because she was going to return the paints when it was all over. It was just winning the bet, and beating Archie. And then Archie would have to stop conning kids at Camp Shady Brook forever. Viewed in that light, conning Sasha was almost a good deed, right?

She just had to keep telling herself that.

ARCHIE

The third week of camp at Shady Brook meant one thing: Parents' Day.

Parents' Weekend was a beloved tradition at other summer camps—or so Archie had heard. But that wasn't the case at Camp Shady Brook. For one, the parents' visit wasn't even on a weekend—it was one day, a Wednesday, smack in the middle of the workweek for most parents and so a colossal hassle for everyone involved.

Archie suspected Miss Hiss liked it that way.

The event was a relic, dating back to the old days when the Beaumonts ran the camp and most kids came for the whole summer instead of one forlorn week in the middle of a summer filled with other activities. Three-quarters of the kids never even got to experience its admittedly limited delights. Archie wasn't sure why they kept doing it—at any rate, his parents never made it up to Vermont to visit, and he was fine with that. It left him free to explore other options.

And there were many of them.

One major benefit of Camp Shady Brook's "Parents' Day," as pathetic and underattended as it was, was the way most of the kids ended the day loaded up with money, candy, magazines, and other treats, all ripe for the picking. Even the campers who didn't have visitors often received especially large care packages from guilty parents who hadn't been able to make the trek.

"Christmas is coming early this year," Archie whispered with a smile to Oliver, while he waited for the painfully slow CITs to dish out that morning's breakfast. Pancakes and fruit. The campers always got fruit on Parents' Day, because the kinds of parents who actually came to visit were usually the kind who would ask their beloved spawn if they were eating enough fruit. Miss Hiss liked to head those kinds of concerns off at the pass.

It was for similar reasons that most of the parents were kept corralled in the main hall for their entire visit—no point in letting them get a look at the decrepit bunks and the disgusting lake. It might make them ask questions about how Miss Hiss was spending their money, and Miss Hiss hated questions.

"Christmas comes early every year at Camp Shady Crook," Oliver whispered back, though he didn't smile. Oliver avoided smiling around the other campers. He thought it made him look weak. Though his grim face didn't stop the little kids from using him as a reluctant jungle gym.

"Teddy Bear!" one of them shouted, coming around the serving table to grab his leg. Oliver shook the kid off, grumbling, "You're not supposed to be back here, it's against the rules," and the boy went to his table with a beaming face and a wave at his favorite CIT. Archie tried not to grin. There was something about Oliver that made people like him, as hard as he tried to prove otherwise.

All around them the campers were buzzing with an unusually high level of energy for a Camp Shady Brook morning. Even the kids who knew they weren't getting any visitors seemed caught up in the excitement of the day.

Oliver grunted. "You can't get distracted by the small stuff today, even if the parents are coming," he said. "You're the one who agreed to this stupid bet. And now you have to keep your eyes on the prize if we're going to get Vivian off our backs."

To prove his point he glared at Mitchell, who was talking excitedly with some of his friends at one of the tables.

"I know, I know," Archie said, looking around to

make sure no one was listening. But he was the only person in line, and the other CITs who were serving were over in the corner, gathering more packets of syrup and giggling about some inside joke. "Besides, tonight is a perfect day to get into the office and put my plan into motion. You know how Miss Hiss is after the parents' visit. She'll be holed up in her house five minutes after they leave."

Unlike the rest of the counselors and staff, Miss Hiss didn't live at the camp proper. Instead she had a whole house to herself, up on the hill where it loomed over the camp in the same ominous way the director loomed over everything the campers did. Meeting parents usually gave her a terrible headache, and as soon as the last car left the parking lot Archie knew she would hightail it for her house, which was rumored to have ice-cold air-conditioning and a seventy-five-inch flat-screen TV.

Oliver nodded, and with a glance at his fellow servers to make sure they were still distracted, slid some extra bacon onto Archie's plate.

After breakfast Archie took a banana and wandered out to the parking lot. He liked to get a sense of what the Parents' Day pickings would be like by checking out the cars. Electric-powered car with SAVE THE EARTH stickers? That kid would have nothing but trail mix. Bor-ing. Flashy sports car? Guaranteed to be filled with a ton of candy. Low-key but obviously expensive sedan? Archie smiled when he spotted one make its way up the rocky dirt road, because he knew that's where you could find the kids who would end the day with loads of cash, just waiting for a well-placed con to take it from them.

As he watched, parents drove up and parked and either stood around for a moment, uncertain, or rushed to meet a kid who was already waiting by the main building. Miss Hiss appeared from her office with a clipboard. "Campers!" she announced. "If your parents have arrived I need you to check in here with me before you go anywhere else on the grounds, is that understood?" She paused, then shouted even louder, "I said, is that understood?"

Ms. Hess always tried mightily to appear less foreboding when the parents were around, and most of them seemed to be fooled—she came off as strict, but kind, and probably most important to the parents, in control. Only the kids knew better.

The parking lot was an excited mass of happy reunions. One set of parents had brought the family dog, which barked frantically, causing Miss Hiss to redden, a vein throbbing in her forehead. Archie suspected that the camper whose family brought that dog would be cleaning the cabin toilets for the rest of the week. Other families had taken along younger siblings, who chased each other around with glee. Hugs and squealed greetings were everywhere, and along with them, ideas for scams that were coming faster than Archie could make mental notes. He knew he wasn't supposed to get distracted—he'd promised Oliver—but something about the mass of excited campers had him feeling like Old Archie more than he had all summer.

Not to mention that Miss Hiss's growing stress level meant that even after the parents left, Archie could look forward to putting in motion his biggest con yet, the one that would solve everything. It felt like the first day of camp all over again, before he'd met Cupcake Girl and had his summer practically ruined. But viewing the scene, he felt back to his old self, and ready to win, once and for all.

Amid all the chaos and his own happy thoughts, Archie was shocked to hear someone call his name.

"Archie?" the voice called again.

He turned and nearly spat out his mouthful of banana. Standing in front of her rusty and ancient Toyota stood his stepmom, Alicia. And in the dirt at her feet, smiling and waving madly like only three-year-olds can, were both of the twins.

VIVIAN

Vivian's parents weren't coming for Parents' Day, since they were on the other side of the world, probably taking a cable car to the top of the Great Wall or doing something else totally awesome and unforgettable. She missed them, of course, but it wasn't like she had expected them to show up.

It wasn't like she was disappointed or anything.

But all the distractions for everyone else made it the perfect day for her to get into the storeroom in the arts and crafts cabin and take those paints for Sasha. Once she had them in hand, she'd get Sasha's fifty dollars and be waving it in Archie's face by the end of the day.

Honestly, taking Archie down a few pegs was just as important as winning the bet. That's why she'd made those well-placed comments to Boring

Janet. She knew her counselor had a huge crush on Mick, the college student who oversaw the Walleyes. Vivian figured Janet would jump at any chance to talk to him privately, especially with concerns about one of his charges. How homesick he was. How devastated he felt that his parents wouldn't be visiting. "I don't know who else to talk to about this," Vivian had confided to Janet. "But I think he really, really needs them to come. It's . . . important."

Like the other campers without parents visiting, she was free for most of the morning, so she came down to the parking lot to check out the families as they arrived. Once everyone was busy she'd just find a quiet moment and put her plan into action. She needed to make sure that Amanda was out of the arts and crafts cabin, and that no campers would barge in at an unfortunate moment. But she also knew Amanda tended to lock up when she wasn't there, so that presented a definite complication. Maybe she needed to find Amanda's keys . . . or come up with a ruse that would get her rushing out without double-checking the doors to the storage room.

As she stared out into the groups of arriving parents, lost in thought, something caught her eye.

It was Archie. But he didn't look like his usual confident self. Or even the shy, awkward persona he put on when he was trying to convince their fellow campers he should be trusted. No, he looked more like he wanted to sink into the earth and disappear. Vivian was well acquainted with that feeling, but it was a look she'd never seen on Archie's face before.

A quick appraisal of the situation told Vivian why. There was a woman with him—she had to be at least thirty-five but she was dressed in shorts and a tank top like one of the campers. The car she'd arrived in was a dusty blue and had rust spots around the wheels, and a window patched with plastic and duct tape. Two toddlers played in the dust at her feet as she talked with Archie.

Well now, Vivian thought to herself. The only reason she'd told the counselors Archie was homesick and needed a visit from his family was to get him out of her hair for most of the day. But if these were the people who had shown up, her plan was turning out even better than she could have hoped.

ARCHIE

What are you doing here?" Archie hissed at his stepmother. One of the twins—they were named Bryce and Aubrey but he could only ever think of them as "the twins"—had something on its face. He thought it was the girl one, but he wasn't sure, since they were dressed in matching clothes. For some reason Alicia thought that was cute. Archie, however, was completely opposed to cute in all forms, toddler or otherwise.

"We came to see you!" Alicia said loudly. Too loudly. He looked around in panic. If anyone caught sight of Alicia they'd know in a minute that he wasn't a rich kid like he'd been pretending to be for weeks. So much of his summer hinged on people thinking his family was mysterious and wealthy, and possibly even famous.

And now here was Alicia, frazzled and wearing

flip-flops and shorts, her hair in a messy bun. She looked like the average mom, but younger, and far from the sophisticated and glamorous movie-star type he pretended his mother was to everyone at camp.

Everything Archie tried to pretend his family wasn't, here in full force and in front of everyone.

It wasn't that he didn't like Alicia. She was okay. She always made him grilled cheese sandwiches when he was sick and made sure he had new clothes for school even when his dad grumbled about the cost. Last year she bought him a pair of sneakers that probably cost a hundred dollars, and told him to tell his dad they'd gotten them on sale. It wasn't her fault—she was who she was. It was just that Archie didn't want to be like her.

At least not here, at Camp Shady Crook.

His mind raced. Maybe he would tell people she was his old nanny? Come to visit him at camp? Or a poor relation. Or his black sheep older sister who had been disowned for marrying the pool boy. Or, or.

"Come say hello to your brother and sister," Alicia said with a big grin. One of the campers from the Rainbow Smelts' cabin who was standing nearby glanced over with a questioning expression.

"Hello," Archie said through gritted teeth. "Come on, let's go." He turned and tried to herd his family away from the crowd, toward the far side of the main camp building, even though he knew the campers were supposed to keep their parents as close to the main hall as possible—primarily so they could stay under the watchful eyes of Miss Hiss. But he needed time to think. What if Mitchell saw her? Mitchell wasn't stupid. He'd have a ton of questions about who Archie really was, and who he'd been claiming to be, and his big con would fall to pieces before he even got started.

"I thought that lady over there said we needed to check in?" Alicia wondered, but Archie ignored her. "And where are we going? I can't walk on dirt in these shoes!"

"I'm giving you a tour, of course," he said grimly. "Isn't that why you're here? To see the place?"

Alicia had one toddler in her arms but the other one was lagging behind, picking up rocks and leaves and examining each one placidly, as though he had all the time in the world.

"Come on, let's go!" Archie said. He had to get them away from the other kids before more people started to notice and ask questions. "Why is he walking so slow?"

"Archie," Alicia said, this time with more than a hint of frustration in her voice. "He's only three. Give him a break, would you?"

Archie clenched and unclenched his fists. Then he walked over to his little brother, picked him up, and began to carry the boy quickly down the path. "I think I'll show you the lake first," Archie said over his shoulder, trying to keep his voice pleasant and calm. "No one will be there this time of day."

Or at least I hope not, Archie thought.

He led his family the long way around the lake, toward the old boathouse. Nobody was supposed to go back there, so it meant he could he get his family away from everyone else while he figured out a plan.

The "new" boathouse, closer to the cabins, was ugly and rusted and looked like a stack of shipping containers left to rot by the docks in Elizabeth, New Jersey. Meanwhile the old boathouse had high arches and was full of rustic charm and the smell of old wood. Of course, it was also notoriously full of bees, which was why nobody ever went near it.

"This is very nice," Alicia said as they examined the building. The sounds of the campers greeting their parents had already faded into the distance. "Sort of like exactly how I pictured summer camp."

She paused. "But what about your friends, Arch? Can't we meet them?" her eyes narrowed. "Or don't you have any friends?"

He thought her tone was more mocking than motherly. She always seemed to care about things like him having friends, and having fun, as though he didn't have more important stuff to do. He knew

Alicia was trying to be nice, but it felt like pressure. She wanted him to be "happy" and "content," but she had no idea what that actually meant for a kid like him. And yet, she'd also driven all the way to Vermont from New Jersey with two toddlers, just to spend an afternoon with him and make sure he was okay. Which only made him feel even more rotten about how much he really, firmly wished she hadn't come.

And she didn't seem to notice the way the sound of buzzing increased the closer they came to the old boathouse. He was hoping she wouldn't get close enough to notice the bees, because she'd insist on going back to the main part of camp immediately. He just needed them to hang out here long enough for him to decide what to do next.

He just needed time to think.

Archie cringed when one of the twins—the girl one, Aubrey—headed right inside the small building and immediately went to investigate a dark corner. He waved his hands frantically at her to come out.

"You can meet my friends later," he said. "They're all with their families now, anyway. It is Parents' Day, right? I mean, that's why you're here?"

"Fabulous, I can't wait," she said. "Because I don't want to have to go back and tell your father you've been sitting in a cabin all summer coming up with your little schemes instead of playing with the other kids, you know. Especially after that e-mail we got."

"What e-mail?" he asked, shocked. But she didn't answer, because without warning, there was a troubling shout from little Aubrey, and the low buzzing that emanated from the boathouse suddenly sounded ten times louder and about a thousand times angrier. "Run!" Archie yelled, pushing his little brother in front of him and trying to get him to hurry up the hill back to the main part of camp where the rest of the campers and their parents were still milling around.

But before he got more than a few feet away, he realized his little sister was still in the boathouse, crying, while Alicia just stood outside, shocked. "Take Bryce!" he shouted at her, which snapped her out of her trance. She grabbed her son and headed up the hill, while Archie darted inside the building, covering his head with his hands until he could reach his little sister, scoop her up, and run as fast as possible outside and up the hill to Alicia.

He handed his stepmother the screaming toddler, then collapsed on the ground, wheezing from the effort of running and batting at the bees that still clung to him. Kids and parents gasped in shock and dismay. Already, Archie's arms and legs were blossoming into angry red marks. His body was in agony, but his mind was even worse.

If he'd been trying to avoid attracting attention to his visiting family, this was definitely not the way to do it.

VIVIAN

After Vivian watched Archie drag his family away from the crowd, she debated following. Part of her wanted to find out what kind of dirt she could get on him. But another part of her was worried.

He looked so unhappy. She'd never seen that expression on his face before, and it made her wonder if there was more to Archie than she'd thought.

But she shook that thought out of her mind. She had a job to do.

Miss Hiss was out in front of her office with her clipboard, giving orders in a low, clipped tone, and all the counselors were scurrying around like a pack of worker ants under her commands, corralling parents and kids and keeping them in the approved areas. She wouldn't actually do anything abusive under the watchful eyes of the parents who paid the bills, but everything about her demeanor suggested only barely repressed violence.

To avoid her, Vivian ducked around the main building toward the arts and crafts cabin and saw Amanda walking out the door.

"Um, hi?" Vivian called, as sweetly as possible. Amanda turned at the sound of her voice, the door to the arts and crafts cabin still open behind her.

"Hi, Vivian, what are you up to?"

Vivian walked up to her and shrugged. "Nothing, really," she said. "I mean, my parents aren't coming today, so . . ."

Amanda smiled at her, and when she spoke there was pity in her voice. "That's got to be tough."

"It's okay," Vivian said. "They're traveling, so I knew they wouldn't be able to come. I just . . ."

"I guess there's not much to do around here today if your parents aren't here," Amanda said. "But I think Ms. Hess is planning on the kids giving a swim demonstration later—you can do that, even if you're on your own."

"I know, but that's not until after lunch," Vivian said, and kicked at a clod of dirt. "I guess I was just wondering if I could get some stuff to make bracelets, or something? Just to kill some time."

Amanda nodded. "I guess so," she said, looking over her shoulder into the arts and crafts cabin.

"But I need to get out front. I'm supposed to be meeting the parents—"

"I'll be quick, I promise!" Vivian said. "And I'll make sure the door is locked when I leave."

Amanda paused, then smiled again. "Well, I'm not supposed to let kids in there unattended, but if you promise you'll just be a minute, it's probably okay."

Vivian beamed at her. "Thank you so much!"

Amanda held the door open for her. "The door will lock behind you once you leave, just make sure it's pulled shut."

"I understand," Vivian said.

She gave Amanda another big smile, and then walked into the empty arts and crafts cabin. The lights were off, and it was dim, but she already knew where she needed to go. First, she grabbed some embroidery floss, without even looking at the colors. It was her cover story, after all. Then she quickly walked to the back storeroom, where Amanda kept the nicest art supplies. It was unlocked, with just an old screen door covering it like the ones on the bunks. Stepping inside she could see metal shelves that held paints, clay, and other art materials. There was sculpting clay, the kind you use to make real sculptures, and all sorts of fabric and markers, the nice kind, not the cheap ones they used most of the time at Camp Shady Crook. And there, on a shelf toward the back, was a stack of paint kits. She opened the one on top—it was filled with beautiful, untouched tubes of paints, all in a little silver suitcase, with brushes and a palette and everything.

Vivian snapped the case shut and then briefly wondered what all this stuff was for, if the campers were never allowed to use it. Amanda always said there wasn't enough to go around, which was why when a kid wandered back here to get crayons or some extra construction paper they were forbidden to take any of the higher-quality supplies. But there was plenty here, even if some of the boxes were old and a little dusty. It seemed unfair, really, that kids who liked art as much as Sasha could never use this stuff.

But Vivian didn't have time to contemplate the inner workings of Camp Shady Crook. She had a job to do. She examined the stack of paint kits. There were only five of them, and she didn't want Amanda to notice one was missing, especially right after Vivian had been in the arts and crafts cabin alone. But they were half hidden behind a box marked BLICK ART MATERIALS, and so with a little shoving, she was able to take a paint kit and then move the box so it hid the rest of them almost completely.

But the box of paints was large, and, she realized, extremely conspicuous. There was no way she was going to get it back to her cabin undetected, even with most of the campers distracted by the visiting families.

So close to winning the bet, and now a camp full of people stood between her and the Rainbow Smelts cabin, and all of them would definitely notice her carrying a large silver case. Plus, if Amanda came back and found it missing, she'd know instantly it was Vivian who took the paints. She was the only kid who had been alone in the arts and crafts cabin, after all. Getting caught by a counselor before she even won the bet was not at all part of her plan.

That's when she spotted the small window at the back of the storeroom. It was closed with one of those old-fashioned flip locks, and, once she tried to lift the sash, she realized it probably hadn't been opened in years. But she finally pried the window open, and then moved it up and down until it slid freely. Then she closed it very carefully so that only a small opening remained—just enough for her to get her fingers in from the other side.

She'd wait until dark, sneak out, and then come in through the window and get the paints. Even if Amanda figured out they were missing, she'd have no way of connecting the crime to Vivian. She gave a shiver of pleasure at her own ingenuity, which only partly masked the uncomfortable feeling she had about stealing something that was valuable enough they didn't let any of the campers touch it. Even if she didn't completely understand Miss Hiss's motivation. Honestly, it was almost like the whole camp was a con bigger than even she could contemplate.

Leaving the window just open enough, she walked out of the storeroom, grabbed the embroidery floss she'd left haphazardly on one of the tables, and let herself out of the cabin, closing the door carefully behind her until the lock clicked.

Once the parents had all left and the tired campers had returned to their cabins for the night, she would go back through the window, grab the paint case, and then bring it to Sasha. The bet was as good as won.

There was a part of her brain that still worried about actually stealing something, but as she kept reminding herself, it was for a good cause. As soon as she won the bet, she'd come clean to Sasha and put the paints back. She'd have beaten Archie and gotten back on top, Sasha would still want to be her friend, and nobody—not Amanda, and definitely not Miss Hiss—would be the wiser.

ARCHIE

Archie was in misery, and not just from the bee stings that dotted his arms, legs, face, and beyond. (There was even one on the top of his head.)

But all he'd wanted to do today was avoid attracting attention to his family. And now, thanks to his own stupidity, the whole camp was abuzz—he winced at the pun even as it formed in his brain—with the story of his adventure with the bees.

"Is that Archie's mom?" he'd heard people whisper as he was half carried, half dragged to the infirmary by a couple of the bigger CITs, Alicia trailing behind with the twins.

"Really?" someone else said. "She doesn't look at all like I thought she would look. I wonder what that's all about."

By the time he got out of the infirmary the news of Alicia's visit would be all over the camp. He needed damage control, and pronto.

Lying in a bed in the small room just off the nurse's office, he contemplated his choices. He'd have to come out in front of this one, like a candidate for office caught in some sort of shady deal. He needed to have a story ready to go the minute he was sent back to his cabin. Something that made sense—maybe that Alicia was his father's secretary? Something logical, but simple enough to be carried through the camp grapevine as quickly as possible, before the truth drowned out whatever story he came up with.

The one thing he really didn't want to think about was what his stepmother had said to him before she took the twins off to the mess hall for lunch.

"Look, I'm proud of you for saving your sister. That was a good thing to do. But I still don't understand why you dragged us back there in the first place. Are you . . . ashamed of us, Arch?"

"No, of course not." Because that wasn't it. Not really. Alicia was . . . fine, most of the time. It was more that they didn't fit into the image of himself that he was trying to project. It wasn't them. It was him. He just didn't want to be boring old Archie Drake from Trenton, was that so wrong? He wanted to be more than he was. Didn't everyone?

The sooner they went home and he was able to weave a believable story about who they were and why they were there, the better.

His frenetic thoughts were interrupted by voices from the main part of the nurse's office. He hadn't given the nurse much consideration before—he was new this year, just like most of the other counselors, and only remotely interesting because he was young and male. The last nurse had been about 110 years old, by most of the campers' estimates, and about as comforting as a boulder. This new nurse, Jack, decorated the infirmary with prints of waterfalls and interesting rock formations and had covered the lumpy cot in the back room with a fuzzy fleece blanket and a pile of fluffy pillows.

But it wasn't Jack talking that Archie heard. Instead, he immediately recognized the angry tone of Miss Hiss in full ranting form. The volume of her voice nearly shook the cabin's cedar walls.

"Fine, he saved his family from getting stung by bees," she was saying to Jack, not bothering to keep her voice down even though the door to the room where Archie lay was half open. "But what I want to know is why was he back there in the first place? Campers aren't supposed to go to the old boathouse. It's completely out of bounds."

"Out of bounds . . . because it's infested with bees?" Jack replied in a more forceful way than

Archie would have expected. It was a stronger tone than practically anyone ever used with Miss Hiss, even the small number of counselors and staff who had been around for years.

"How was I to know that old building was harboring pests? I never go up there, myself. There's no need. Nobody's been back there for years."

"Maybe because it's been *like* that for years? People talk, you know," Jack said. "And I can't understand why you haven't had a service out to move the hives before now. It's clearly a danger to the campers to have so many bees near where they live and play. It's a huge hazard; you have to see that."

Miss Hiss's voice took on an icy sheen. "I know this is your first summer here, Jack, but you must realize, this camp isn't made of money. The Beaumonts always insist on bringing in scholarship students like this problem child, Mr. Drake, and it's become increasingly difficult to fund the most basic amenities."

"But this is a safety issue!" Jack said. "It's about the health of the campers. Their parents trust us with them. And if that doesn't bother you, maybe the fact that dozens of parents were here today and got to see this whole episode play out right in front of their eyes will. I'm sure they're going to have lots of questions about what you plan to do to make sure it doesn't happen again."

Miss Hiss grunted. "Okay, fine. I'll look into doing . . . something about the bees. But that doesn't have anything to do with the immediate problem. What do we do with Mr. Drake in there?"

"What do we do with him? Well, I've removed all the stingers, but he'll need cold compresses and maybe some medication. Luckily it doesn't look like he's severely allergic. But I'll keep him here until after dinner, just in case, and get him some lotion to help with the itching."

"I don't mean about his bee stings," Miss Hiss spat. "I mean about his behavior. Clearly he feels comfortable going out of bounds if he took his whole family out to that horrible old boathouse only a few minutes after they arrived. I can only imagine how often he's been breaking rules when he's by himself with no supervision. That new Walleyes counselor is worthless."

Her voice lowered. "In fact, I received a letter from a very angry set of parents last week who said their son—Julian Eubanks, is his name—was conned out of fifty dollars by this boy, Archie Drake."

In the bed in the rear room, Archie gulped.

As if this day couldn't get any worse.

"That's a pretty serious accusation," Jack said. "What are you trying to say?"

Miss Hiss laughed, but it wasn't a humorous sound. "What I'm trying to say is I think that boy needs to be watched. Very, very closely."

Miss Hiss walked over to the back room where Archie lay and glanced around the door. He squeezed his eyes shut and pretended he was asleep. She closed the door carefully, without making any noise. Archie had to strain to hear what she said next.

"It's clear to me that Archie Drake is trouble. But I'm not going to give him a couple of demerits, oh no. I'm going to catch him red-handed, mark my words. And then he'll be out of Camp Shady Brook so fast, his head will spin."

Archie winced in pain, and not from the welts all over his body. Attracting Miss Hiss's attention was even worse than the rumors he was sure were spreading like wildfire among the other campers. And if she knew what had happened with Julian . . . then it was only a matter of time before everything fell apart.

Which meant he had to make his big play as soon as possible. Or else Cupcake Girl would win. And that was worse than any amount of bee stings.

He leaned back into the pile of pillows and tried to avoid thinking of the itching, and of the uncomfortable feelings he was having about the day, and about his family, and most of all, about what Alicia had said about him being ashamed of them. But both sensations were becoming more and more impossible to ignore.

VIVIAN

When the news reached Vivian, she felt a small twinge of sympathy before the glee set in. She'd been stung by a bee once, in Central Park, while she was just sitting by herself under a tree. The little buzzer had come out of nowhere, and she'd ended up walking all by herself to the drugstore to buy medicine since her parents were at work, as usual. Even with the medication, the bite had been itchy and swollen for a week.

She couldn't imagine how badly it would hurt to be stung as many times as Archie was. The whole camp was talking about it. "A hundred times," one of the Rainbow Smelts said that night at dinner. "He was stung all over his body!"

Still, if Vivian wanted to win their bet, she had to push that feeling of sympathy as far down as possible and think about strategy instead. Already

her well-placed comments about his homesickness
had led to better results than she had ever expected.
So she had to think how she could use this latest
setback to her advantage. Archie may have considered himself the chess master, but it was his over-
confidence that would be his downfall, she was sure
of it.

She'd guessed right that any parents, hearing
how homesick their kid was — and from a counselor,
no less — would be sure to come for Parents' Day.
Even all the way from South Jersey. But she'd only
hoped the unexpected visit would keep him busy
all day, not land him in the infirmary as the camp's
most-talked-about patient a half hour after the
families arrived.

Still, she knew if she'd been handed a chance
like this one, she had to grab it.

That night, once the Rainbow Smelts were
settled into their bunks, she waited patiently until
she could hear the breathing of all of her fellow
campers grow slower, the whispers and giggles
fading into nothingness and sleep. She willed
herself to stay awake, pinching the inside of her
upper arm every time she felt herself dozing off.
Once she was convinced everyone else was finally
sleeping, she slowly shifted herself out of bed, trying in vain to keep the rickety bunk from creaking
or shaking.

"Vivian?" Sasha's sleepy voice drifted down from the top bunk. "Is that you?"

Great, Vivian thought. *This is exactly what I need.* She tried to keep the displeasure out of her voice. "Just going to the bathroom."

"Oh, are you okay? Are you sick or something?"

"I'm fine, Sash, just go back to sleep."

Sasha didn't answer. Vivian hoped she'd fallen back asleep. As stealthily as she could, she stood up from the bunk and slipped out through the broken screen in the cabin's front door without opening it. At least that was one benefit of that door, even if it did let in armies of mosquitoes.

Once she was outside in the cool night air, she let out her breath. She hadn't realized she'd been holding it since Sasha spoke. Then as quickly as she could walk without making any noise, she headed down the path to the arts and crafts cabin. She'd already plotted out a route that kept her away from any of the places the counselors might be, like the mess hall or the infirmary.

This is going to be easier than I thought it would be, she thought to herself as she ducked behind the bushes under the back window of the arts and crafts cabin. All she had to do was push open the window, climb through, get the paints, and then make it back to her bed before anyone noticed she was gone.

She'd just begun to ease open the window—it was sticky, and a bit higher up on the outside than it had been when she'd opened it earlier in the day—when she saw motion out of the corner of her eye. A boy, his face in shadows from the trees. But that didn't matter. She knew that boy.

It was Oliver, Archie's not-so-little sidekick.

Without thinking, she ran.

ARCHIE

After lights out, Archie quietly pulled his shoes from under the end of his bed, and tiptoed out of the Walleyes' cabin. He held his breath as he eased open the creaky screen door, but none of his bunkmates budged. They were all fast asleep. He'd convinced Nurse Jack to let him come back to his bunk after dinner, but even without the plans he needed to put in motion, he was sure he'd never sleep. Too itchy. Besides, he wasn't at all sure his cabinmates had believed the story he'd told about Alicia. All the more reason to win this bet, and fast.

As soon as he reached the bottom of the front steps he shoved his feet into his sneakers and then, with a quick look to the right and left, headed for the main office, keeping well into the shadows and away from the lighted parts of the path.

Oliver was already there, nearly invisible under a tree around the corner from the door. Archie gave him a thumbs-up and then, standing as close to the building as he could without touching it, slid his body around the side of the main office and peered in the window next to the door. Nobody was inside, and the lights were out. Another thumbs-up, then he quickly darted around the back of the building where there weren't any windows. However, there was a service door next to the camp store that had a flimsy, easy-to-jiggle-open lock. A few tense moments later, he was inside.

He allowed himself a minute to let his eyes adjust to the darkness and willed himself to ignore the horrible itching of the bee stings. Without the moonlight it was almost pitch-black, but Archie didn't mind. The less light, the less likely someone would see him or what he was about to do.

He was in the short hallway that divided Miss Hiss's spacious office from the even larger camp store. She often walked across the way to grab pens, or a snack—unlike the campers, her credit was excellent there. But he knew the store would be locked up tight at this hour. Miss Hiss's office, however, opened directly onto the hall, with a large archway that allowed her to watch the comings and goings of the store staff with intense efficiency.

Once in the office he took a quick look around—

the temptation to snoop was immense, though he knew that she kept her most important files up in the house on the hill, where she was undoubtedly nursing the headache she always got on Parents' Day. He liked to think that despite the personal horrors of the day, he'd at least contributed a small part to that. He smiled to himself at the thought, for what seemed like the first time in eons.

Alicia had been kind enough, when she and the twins had said good-bye that afternoon. But he could see the hurt in her eyes.

The walls around Miss Hiss's desk were covered with awards and photos from her days as the director of the biggest chain of camps in New England. In the most prominent place was a large plaque, dark wood with a brass plate on the front that was inscribed, CAMP DIRECTOR OF THE YEAR, PHILO- MENA HESS. Archie briefly wondered what had changed for Miss Hiss, how she had fallen so far. One day, winning awards, the next day, in charge of the worst camp in Vermont. No wonder she was so angry all the time.

But he didn't have time to ruminate on Miss Hiss's failed career trajectory. So he sat down on her desk chair and quickly started up her computer. Which immediately asked for a password.

Archie said a word he wasn't normally allowed to say around his father.

Or at school. Or anywhere, really. The computer hadn't needed a password the year before, when he and Oliver had first figured out they could get into the office at night.

With mounting panic, he considered the situation. The pain and itching from the bug bites made it hard to concentrate. But, he reasoned, Miss Hiss wasn't someone who loved computers or any other type of technology. Her attitude toward kids having access to anything of the sort at camp made that abundantly clear. In some ways, she reminded him of his stepmother—Alicia loved her phone when it worked, but was completely mystified by it and called it names when it didn't. And one of the things his stepmother hated the most was remembering passwords.

So instead of actually committing them to unreliable memory, she always kept hers on a list . . . right inside the top drawer of the desk in their kitchen. He'd used that list himself, once or twice, when he was curious about the family finances.

With a sudden burst of inspiration, Archie pulled open the top drawer of Miss Hiss's desk, and, bingo. A piece of paper was taped right inside, with a list of words and phrases.

"ShadyBrook1" was the first one. *Really?* he thought to himself. *What's the point of having a password at all if that's what you're going to pick? She might as well have picked "password."*

But he didn't really have anything to complain about, because the password worked on the first try. He started up the Web browser and quickly got to work.

First he needed to print out an old-timey treasure map. It didn't really matter what it was—by the time his plan was in motion, it would be fine if it was a map of the Ozarks. Just as long as it looked old. But the second piece of his plan would take a little more work. He went to a website he'd found at home one day where you could make fake newspaper clippings. They weren't all that realistic looking, but it would work for something that was supposed to look like it was printed off the Internet. He carefully copied the text he'd written on a piece of paper earlier, and then used the formatting tools to make it look just right.

Sitting there in the darkness working on the computer, with the clock on the wall ticking ominously behind him, he felt like a superspy. Or a master criminal. If a master criminal would be sitting at a computer covered in bee stings and pink anti-itch lotion.

After another quick read-through of his work, he hit print and the surprisingly high-quality printer in the corner sprang to life.

And almost immediately started beeping and flashing a red light.

Error, it said. *Error.*

Archie sighed. For a moment he'd almost felt like James Bond. But he suspected James Bond never had to deal with paper jams.

Once he'd manhandled the printer into submission he printed out his map and fake news clipping and looked them over. They looked pretty professional, even in the dim light of the computer screen.

And that's when he heard Oliver's signal. "Caw, caw."

Archie stood straight up from the desk. He quickly shut down the Web browser and the computer and, willing himself to stay calm, grabbed his papers and bolted out of the office. Then he and Oliver ran as quietly as they could, hearts pounding, back to the cabins.

"Who was it?" Archie whispered once they had stopped, a few yards away from the Walleyes' cabin. They rested in the shadows to catch their breath.

"I don't know," Oliver said, still panting from the run. "I just heard something. And then I saw someone—out behind the arts and crafts cabin."

"Who?"

"I don't know," Oliver said. "A kid. But it was so dark, I couldn't see his face. Whoever it was, they spotted me and ran, then I panicked and gave the signal."

"It's okay," Archie said. "You were just being careful. That's what you get paid to do."

Oliver gave him a small smile. "Did you get everything?"

"Yeah," Archie replied, waving the papers in his hand. All present and accounted for. Honestly, he wasn't all that concerned about some strange kid lurking around the arts and crafts cabin.

Because it was finally time to con Mitchell the Unconnable.

VIVIAN

The next morning Vivian woke up thinking about her failure of the night before. She was tired and cranky and she had a headache, and Sasha was no help at all.

"So, did you get those paints?" Sasha asked quietly—for Sasha—as they were brushing their teeth in front of the cracked mirror in the cabin bathroom. "I've been thinking nonstop about what I want to paint first!"

Vivian tried to sound cheerful. "Today!" she said. "I'll get them for you today. You've got the money, right?"

"Well, yeah?" Sasha replied. "I mean, it's in my cubby? I haven't spent any of it yet because the stuff at the camp store is just so expensive! Though I'd like to see the paints first, you know? Make sure they are worth it! I mean, a lot of people think they know about paints and what's good, but they don't always know and I kind of do, you know, so I don't want to be a pain, but?"

Vivian had stopped listening. Her mind was already working on Plan B.

Sneaking out at night wasn't the best plan. She hadn't expected to see Oliver, of all people, lurking around the main camp buildings after hours.

With a start, she realized that he probably wasn't just hanging out for fun—he was doing something. Something with Archie. Something to win the bet.

Which only meant she had to get those paints into Sasha's hands as soon as possible.

Vivian found her chance later that day.

"Hey, I don't feel so good," she told Sasha and Lily and the rest of the Rainbow Smelts as they walked to swim lessons. "I think I need to go to the nurse. Tell Janet for me, okay?"

"Oh gosh, I hope you're not really sick!" Sasha said. "You were up last night, right? Is it your stomach?"

Vivian had hoped Sasha had forgotten the little interlude from the night before, but no such luck. Still, it gave her an easy excuse, and she jumped at it. "Yeah, my stomach has been bugging me since yesterday," she said. "I'll go talk to Nurse Jack. Maybe he can give me some medicine or something."

Sasha frowned. "I hope it's not anything contagious!"

"Probably just something I ate. You know how Camp Shady Crook food—I mean, Camp Shady Brook food—is hard on the digestive system," Vivian said in what she hoped was a reassuring tone. "Don't worry about me. I'll catch you later."

She dropped back from the group and headed slowly toward the infirmary. But once the girls were far enough down the path to no longer see her, her pace quickened, until she was once again in the bushes behind the arts and crafts cabin. *It's now or never*, she thought to herself.

The window was still ajar, thankfully, so with a few pushes she was able to get it open. She listened carefully and it didn't sound like anyone was in the cabin, so she hoisted herself up—for once thankful for the gymnastics lessons her parents had insisted on her taking—and then into the dim storeroom. All she had to do was grab the paints, climb back through the window, then head to the Rainbow Smelts cabin to hide them. Most of the kids were at the lake now, so if she planned her path correctly, she'd avoid seeing anyone.

The paints were just where she left them, in the stack of boxes on the back shelf. She grabbed the top set, and was headed toward the window when she paused. What if a counselor spotted her carrying them? Someone was always patrolling the paths. How would she explain? She looked quickly around the room. In the corner was a pile of fabric pieces—she ruffled through them until she found one the right size and wrapped it around the box of paints. That way she could tell people she was carrying dirty laundry.

There was a rattling from the main room of the arts and crafts cabin, then the sound of a door opening.

Vivian froze.

"All I'm saying is that the kids are bored! They want to do more than just make friendship bracelets and collages." It was Amanda, and she sounded frustrated.

Then, to Vivian's horror, she heard the unmistakable voice of Miss Hiss. "Those supplies are expensive, Amanda, and I don't want to see them being all used up by a bunch of kids. If you were good at your job"—here, her voice took on an even more menacing tone than usual—"you could keep the campers engaged in any kind of project. I don't see why you need fancy paints and clay."

"But we have all the supplies already in the back room! Just sitting there."

"Yes, and once the kids start using them, then

what happens? We'll have to replace them, and that costs money. Money, I don't like to remind you, that this camp doesn't have."

"But it's just a few art supplies. . . ." Amanda sounded resigned. "Oh well, I guess we could get some macaroni from the kitchen and make beads or something?"

"Wasting good food? I think not," Miss Hiss snapped back. "And I don't have time for this today. I have to take a call from the Beaumonts to update them on how the session is going."

"Oh, about the bees?"

Miss Hiss, well, hissed. "We are *not* telling the Beaumonts about the bees! They have enough to worry about. You know Mr. Beaumont is very ill; that's why they haven't been up here in ages. Just give me the printer paper I asked for, and let me get back to my work. This camp doesn't run itself, you know."

Vivian stood stock-still in the back room, with the box of paints wrapped in fabric still in her arms. What if Amanda came back there? She had to think fast. She quickly moved toward the window and then slid the paint box down the side of the building as far as she could, finally letting it drop once she could no longer hold it. It made a small thud as it bumped against the wood siding and she willed the adults in the other room not to hear. But at least if they found her, they wouldn't find the paints.

Or so she hoped.

"Fine, let me get what you need," Amanda said, sounding resigned, and her footsteps came sickeningly close to the door to the storeroom. But then the steps turned away, and Vivian let out her breath as she realized that the counselor was going to the rack of paper just outside the storeroom door.

But she knew she had to move. She willed her jelly legs to work again and, hoping against all hope that Miss Hiss and Amanda wouldn't hear her, she climbed onto a box, let her feet out the window, then dropped into the dirt next to the box of paints. No time to close the window, not with the screechy wooden frame and the camp director just a few yards away. Instead, she grabbed the box and its haphazard fabric covering and darted away from the cabin toward the bunks. She brushed past a bunch of boys on the path as she ran.

"Hey, watch it," one of them called. But Vivian didn't stop.

ARCHIE

Vivian seemed to be lying low. Or at least she was avoiding Archie.

He wasn't sure how he felt about that.

He was also beginning to suspect the kid Oliver had spotted outside after hours was, in fact, Vivian, which meant she had some sort of plan in the works to win the bet. Of course, he wouldn't have expected anything less. Not from her. His mind teetered from begrudging respect for her skills to annoyance at her insistence she could beat him, that he wasn't the King of Cons. Because if he wasn't that, what was he? That was why he had to win the bet. Not just to beat her, but to prove to her, and to himself, that he was as good at this as he had always thought himself to be. At least before Cupcake Girl came along.

"I think she's up to something," Archie said

quietly as he and Oliver stood, pretending to ignore each other, by the lake. "You need to keep an eye on her."

"Whatever you say, you're the boss," Oliver said. "But—"

"But what?"

"Nothing," Oliver said, and kicked a rock, hard enough that it went flying into the lake and nearly took out the eye of a ten-year-old girl from the Chain Pickerel cabin. The two of them were observing the group's swim lesson from the trees just out of sight of the dock.

They couldn't meet in the woods anymore, not since the bee incident, because that whole area of the camp was blocked off with sawhorses and caution tape, including the archery range and their usual meeting spot.

"I just think it was more fun when we were working together, that's all."

"With Cupcake Girl?" Archie was incredulous. "Would you please stop trying to convince me we were better off working with her? Because that's clearly not true."

"She has a name, you know. Vivian. Vivian Cheng," Oliver said. "And yeah, it was better. Come on, Arch, you know I'm right."

Archie made a face but didn't say anything. It was true that life at Camp Shady Brook had gone downhill dramatically since he began his feud with Cupcake Girl. Sorry, with Vivian. Parents' Day, the bees, and Alicia, to name a few. Maybe some of those things could have been avoided if they'd stuck together instead of trying to scam each other. She was pretty smart, after all. Maybe once he won the bet they could go back to the way things were, at least a little bit.

He just had to get back on top. He was Archie Drake, after all.

"Well, it's too late now to work together whether you want to or not," Archie said. "We've got the bet to think about. And the sooner we win, the sooner all of this is over."

So once the Bluegills and Chain Pickerels were done with their swim lessons, Archie made his big play.

"Mitchell! Hey, Mitch!" he called, and rushed to catch up with the younger boy.

Archie put on his broadest smile and acted like he was out of breath from running. It was an old ploy, a way to make himself seem vulnerable, and put kids at ease before he started weaving his tales.

"Hi, Archie," Mitchell said, looking a little surprised. "What are you doing here? Aren't you in the Walleyes?"

"Yeah," Archie said, ducking his head and making a big show of catching his breath. "But they're busy at arts and crafts right now and I kind of wanted to talk to you."

"To me?"

"About—" Archie paused and lowered his voice, then looked around to make sure the rest of the Bluegills were farther up the path toward the mess hall and couldn't hear their conversation. "Pirates."

"Pirates?" Mitchell's voice got higher and louder. "What about pirates?"

"Shh," Archie said. "This is just between you and me. The thing is, our conversation the other day got me thinking . . . and I remembered my friend back home is into pirates too. And he sent me this letter I totally forgot about until we talked the other day. About how there used to be pirates here, in Vermont."

"That's impossible," Mitchell said.

"I know, it sounds unbelievable, right?" One of Archie's rules was always to agree with the mark. It made them trust him. "But that's what he said. And he sent me this news article to prove it."

Archie pulled the fake article he'd created on the computer out of his pocket. He'd creased it carefully, so it looked like something that had been sent in a letter. Those kinds of details were his specialty. The kind of thing that made even the most implausible story seem just plausible enough. At least for most kids.

Mitchell the Unconnable was, well, a different story.

Still, if Archie was going to win the bet, he had to make the play.

Mitchell examined the article. "The *Vermont Tribune*? Is that a newspaper?"

"I guess so," Archie said. "Just read it."

The news story—which Archie knew by heart, since he'd written it—explained how Bluebottle the Pirate had sailed up the Missisquoi River from Lake Champlain all the way to their own little Lake Joyeaux through a little-known tributary, long since run dry. And better yet, the story continued, he was rumored to have buried his famed treasure near the shore, more than one hundred years ago.

"This is amazing!" Mitchell said, and he sounded more excited than Archie could have hoped. "Where did you get this, again?"

"From my friend at home, he sent it to me, because he knows I'm here at camp," Archie said, with more patience than he felt. "And here's the thing—he says there's a map."

"A map?"

"Yeah, he knows where to get it. A map that will take us directly to the treasure. All we have to do is pay the guy who has it one hundred dollars."

And that was it: the play. Archie smiled, hoping against hope Mitchell would take the bait.

But Mitchell's face fell. "That's a lot of money. I don't have that kind of money."

"But I'll pay half!" Archie said quickly. "And then we can split the treasure. We'll be rich. And famous!"

"But shouldn't we give the map to, like, archeologists or something? We could mess up the whole site, if it's real. It's, like, a historic place."

"No archeologist is going to come here! They won't believe this. It's just a rumor and an old map." Archie tried to keep the frustration out of his voice. Part of what made Mitchell so unconnable was the fact that he was so darn reasonable. He didn't see things the way the other kids did. And that was a problem. Not an unsolvable problem, but a problem all the same.

Mitchell took a deep breath. "Well, let me think about it. It would be cool, to find real pirate treasure. Like, really, really cool. Do you think your friend could send us the map? I mean, before we leave camp?"

His eyes were shining. For a brief moment, Archie felt an unusual-for-him pang of guilt. What must it be like to be someone like Mitchell? Trusting and honest and truly excited about searching for pirate treasure? Instead of convincing people it existed, simply to win a bet?

Archie just nodded. And then with great effort,

he shrugged his shoulders like he didn't care at all, even though the last thing he wanted was for a mark—especially such an irritatingly reasonable and rational one like Mitchell—to spend any serious time actually thinking about his propositions. Nothing fell apart under scrutiny like a con.

But he felt nervous, much more on edge than he usually was. There was just so much riding on this. His entire reputation, for one.

He had to keep it together. He just needed to convince Mitchell that the treasure was really there—and, more important, that he had to act fast, just like they said in TV commercials for kitchen gadgets and skin cream. If Mitchell didn't feel a sense of urgency, Archie would never win the bet.

Archie knew better than to let on what he was really thinking, so he just took a breath and said, "Sure, sure. Take all the time you need." Then he added, forcing himself to make it sound like an afterthought, "Just let me know as soon as possible. I'm pretty sure once word gets out about the map, tons of people will want it. I've already written my friend and told him to send it to me." He paused for a second. "You know . . . I bet it's under the dock, don't you think? I mean, we'll need the map to be sure. But that's what makes the most sense. I bet that dock has been there for at least a hundred years, probably more. If it was any other place it would have probably been forced up during a storm or something."

"You think?" Mitchell said. "Under the dock? But the map will tell us exactly, right?"

"Of course," Archie said smoothly. Mitchell the Unconnable had taken the bait. He couldn't wait to tell Oliver.

"This is so exciting," Mitchell said with a broad smile. "A real-life pirate treasure for us to find. Thanks for telling me first! Really. I mean it."

"No problem," Archie said. "Catch you later." And he walked off, but once he left Mitchell behind, he felt less pleased with himself than he thought he would be. Something about how sincere Mitchell had acted—how he had wondered if the treasure map should be given to archeologists, instead of immediately wanting it for himself—rattled Archie more than he wanted to admit.

It made him think about poor Julian, who had trusted Archie about the candy, and even about Alicia, and how hurt she'd been by Archie's obvious displeasure at her arrival on Parents' Day. He'd always been able to con people because of their faith in him. Only now was he beginning to see just how often he'd squandered that faith for his own ends.

He shook his head hard. *Don't get soft on me now, Archie Drake*, he thought to himself. *Time to focus. Time to win.*

VIVIAN

That evening, during Quiet Time, Vivian widened her eyes at Sasha and pointedly shook her head toward the bathroom.

"What?" Sasha said innocently. "Are you still feeling sick? Do you need help with something? I can hold your hair if you need to throw up, I don't mind!"

It took Vivian a minute to realize what she was talking about. "Um, no, not that—just, well, come *on*," she whispered in frustration. "I need to talk to you."

Once Sasha headed toward the bathroom, Vivian grabbed the paint set, still wrapped in fabric, from where she'd hidden it under her bed. And when they were alone she pulled it out and handed it to Sasha.

"Wow," Sasha breathed, too surprised and

pleased to use her normal exclamation points. "This is, this is amazing. . . ." She put the case on one of the chipped sinks and carefully opened it, running her hands over the tubes of paint, each nestled in its own foam slot. Then she slid a paintbrush from the bands that held them to the inside of the lid. "Look at this!" she said. "These are even nicer than the ones I have at home!"

She turned to Vivian with wide eyes. "Are you sure this is okay? I mean, my parents would be supermad if I sold a paint set like this! It has to have cost a lot more than fifty dollars!"

Vivian shrugged. "All I know is this girl wanted to sell it, and you wanted paints," she said. "I'm just trying to do you a favor here."

Sasha smiled at her, and her smile was so joyful it made Vivian avoid looking her in the eye. "Thank you so much! I don't know how I can ever repay you! This changes my whole summer!"

Vivian coughed, without meaning to. "It's fine," she said a little grumpily. She knew Sasha would be happy but she didn't realize how happy, and now the prospect of having to come clean to her once the bet was over seemed even more difficult. What would Sasha say when she knew the truth? Would she understand it wasn't really a con? Just a way to beat Archie. Not a way to get at Sasha. Not really.

"I have the money, if that's what you're worried

about?" Sasha said. "I'll give it to you after lights out! I mean, I'm sure this girl, whoever she is, really wants it as soon as possible!"

"Yeah, she does," Vivian said. She was so close to winning the bet that she could already visualize the scene tomorrow morning at breakfast when she waved that money in Archie's face. She'd also make sure Archie saw Sasha with the paints, before taking them back and explaining everything.

But she thought she'd be happier, winning. Instead, looking at Sasha, she felt like a fraud. What would it be like to be just a regular friend to Sasha, not someone trying to con her? Just to hang out with her, and do stuff together, like all the other kids?

Maybe once she solved the problem of Archie she could find out. She tried her best to smile back at Sasha. "I'm glad you're happy," she said.

And for all the lies she'd told this summer, that, at least, was the truth.

ARCHIE

When Archie woke up the next morning, the cabin was suspiciously silent. Too silent, especially for a room that was normally packed to the breaking point with twelve-year-old boys.

"Hello?" he called. "Where is everybody?" But no one answered, because he was the only one there. He checked his watch. It was barely 5:30 a.m.

With a vague sense of panic he couldn't identify, Archie pulled on shorts and a T-shirt and, without even brushing his teeth, headed out the front door to find a mass of campers of all ages standing around in front of the cabins and down along the path toward the lake.

"What's going on?" he asked no one in particular.

"Miss Hiss is on a rampage," a boy he didn't know answered. "We're supposed to all meet up in front of the main hall; at least that's what people are saying. All the counselors are there already, but nobody wants to be the first one to go down there. I think Miss Hiss might actually hurt someone this time. My friend said he saw her shove one of the counselors so hard he fell into a tree."

Down the row of cabins, closer to the lake, a shout went up from one of the older girls. "Oh my God, look!" she said in a loud, dramatic voice that begged a response. It was that girl from Vivian's cabin, Lily, with the long hair, the one they'd conned at Field Day the first week. "Look at the dock!"

Half the kids rushed to see what she was pointing at. For Archie, the panic that had started as just a small twinge when he woke up began to grow like a balloon, filling his stomach with air. Even though he'd barely walked ten paces, he felt like he'd run a marathon.

Fighting the lump in his throat, he followed the group headed toward Lily's voice and pushed his way to the front.

The dock—the old, beat-up dock, the only way in and out of the lake without wading through all the weeds—was gone.

He, along with the rest of the campers, stared in disbelief.

But looking more closely, he realized it wasn't

gone entirely. It just wasn't anything resembling a dock anymore.

Pieces of wood, cracked and broken, floated out into the mucky water of Lake Joyless, moving farther and farther from shore by the second.

He sensed the shape of a person beside him. "Oh no." It was Mitchell the Unconnable, and he sounded as distressed as Archie felt. "Oh no."

Archie whirled on him, and whispered fiercely, "What happened? Do you know?"

Mitchell let out a deep sigh that sounded almost like a sob. His face was a mask of horror. "Not really, but I think it's all my fault. I mean, it has to be—because I was talking to some of the boys in my cabin last night, about you know, that thing you were telling me about—" His voiced dropped even lower. "The map."

"You *told* people?" Archie didn't care at this point if anyone heard him. He was too shocked.

"I just wanted their opinions, that's all," Mitchell said.

Typical Mitchell. Archie rolled his eyes. "And then what?"

"Well, we spent all of dinner going over it, you know, where the treasure might be. And one of the guys said if there was really treasure in the lake, then you were probably right, that it was probably under the dock—I mean, that's the only place where it wouldn't have forced its way up to the surface, right? Over a hundred years? Isn't that what you said?"

"I guess so. . . ." Archie said. He only vaguely remembered what he'd said to Mitchell. It was just the sort of stuff he said when he was conning someone. People were only supposed to believe him enough to take the bait. It wasn't supposed to end up like *this*.

"Anyway, some of them—they went out last night and tried to find it. They tried to pry up part of the dock to see what was underneath. And you know it was practically broken anyway. . . . Then this happened. They're lucky nobody got badly hurt, just a few splinters, and one kid scraped up his leg. But they're going to be in massive trouble once Miss Hiss figures out who they are."

Archie put his hand to his head. "I see," he said, trying to sound calmer than the growing balloon in his stomach made him feel.

"I don't think they found anything, if you're wondering about that," Mitchell said. "They would have told me."

"Of course they didn't find anything!" Archie snapped back. "It's just—they—but—" He was too upset to even get the words out.

A crackle of feedback from the camp intercom broke through the murmuring sounds of the other campers. And then, Miss Hiss's voice boomed over the whole camp, sounding more menacing than it ever had before.

"All campers must report to the flagpole immediately. IMMEDIATELY. That means RIGHT NOW."

VIVIAN

Miss Hiss was pacing back and forth in front of her office as the campers assembled in front of the flagpole that stood next to the parking lot, a tattered and limp flag hanging from the top. Her eyes were wild, her hair uncombed. She looked like if she tried hard enough she could shoot fire out of her mouth.

Vivian had gotten out of bed as soon as Janet had rushed out of the cabin—they'd all been woken by a counselor from the Bluegills with a very sharp and loud voice, who had marched into the bunk without knocking and headed straight for Janet's room. "Staff meeting," the counselor had said gruffly. "In five minutes."

All the girls in the cabin could hear Janet's groan.

So once the announcement came over the loudspeaker, Vivian dressed quickly and joined Sasha and the rest of the Rainbow Smelts as the camp director began her tirade.

Even for Miss Hiss, it was a major display of outrage. And that was saying something.

"This is completely unacceptable!" Miss Hiss shouted, loud enough that some of the smaller kids covered their ears. A few looked close to tears. "Willful destruction of property! Campers out after hours! Massive rule violations!"

She whirled on the counselors, who stood huddled to the side of the building, afraid to come any closer to her fury.

"If any of you have anything you need to report to me, anything at all, about the antics going on at this camp, I strongly recommend you come forward this instant—or face the consequences!"

Most of the counselors looked at the ground. But heaving a big sigh, Amanda, the arts and crafts counselor, took a step forward and furtively put up her hand.

"What now?" Miss Hiss said. She seemed shocked that someone had actually responded to her request.

"I'm sorry I didn't tell you before," Amanda said in a loud but robotic voice. "But there have been some items that have gone . . . missing from the arts and crafts storeroom."

Vivian's eyes widened, and her stomach dropped down to her knees.

"Items? What kind of items?"

Amanda sighed and shrugged. "A paint set, for sure. And maybe some fabric. And possibly some other things. I just noticed it last night. I'm not sure when they were taken."

"A paint set?" Miss Hiss asked. "And you didn't come and tell me right away?" She stepped closer to Amanda, who shrank back, as did all the other counselors and campers behind her. Miss Hiss was no longer shouting, but somehow, that just made her voice seem scarier.

"I wanted to make sure they were really gone," Amanda said helplessly. "Double-check that some kids hadn't taken the supplies by accident, or that I hadn't misplaced them."

"Oh really?" Miss Hiss said. "No wonder we've got this kind of behavior at this camp, when we have counselors who are apparently unwilling to inform me about THEFTS of IMPORTANT SUP-PLIES." She stepped so close to Amanda, they were practically nose-to-nose. "That's it—you're fired. Effective immediately."

Amanda looked shocked, as did the rest of the counselors. "But—I didn't do anything. I just told you what happened. Some things are missing—"

"I'm still holding you responsible," Miss Hiss,

well, hissed. "Hand over your keys and get your things. I want you out of here in fifteen minutes or I'm calling the police."

The campers gasped. Amanda's eyebrows rose. "You want the keys?" she asked in a strange voice. "The keys to the arts and crafts cabin?"

"Of course, those keys belong to the camp, and they're the only set we have right now. Hand them over."

Amanda took a deep breath, and then, glancing behind her at the counselors and campers, she gave them all a strange grin and said, "Well, why don't you go and get them?" With a smooth motion she pulled the keys out of her pocket and with an admirable throwing arm, tossed them as far as she could into the woods behind the main building, which were still surrounded by caution tape—thanks to the bee infestation from Parents' Day.

"Good luck," she said, more to the campers than to Miss Hiss. And with that, she just walked toward the parking lot, almost like she taking a casual weekend stroll.

A few counselors looked like they wanted to clap, but then, shooting looks at their boss, clearly thought better of it.

"Come back here!" Miss Hiss shrieked. "You can't do that with camp property, that's—that's . . ."

She didn't finish her thought, but instead whirled

on the group of campers and counselors still huddled around the flagpole. Her voice turned sinister. "I don't know what's going on here, and who is truly responsible for all this chaos, but I have some ideas." Her eyes flitted over the crowd, and maybe it was Vivian's imagination, but they seemed to rest for the longest time on Archie, who was standing only a few feet away. "And I assure you, I assure you I will find out. And when I do . . ."

The unspoken threat hung in the air like smoke from a dying campfire.

Then Miss Hiss wheeled around and walked back into her office, slamming the door so hard that the ancient wooden sign nailed to it that said CAMP SHADY BROOK fell and broke into pieces on the steps.

Vivian didn't want to approach Miss Hiss's office, but she felt a sudden urge to pick up the wooden bits of sign that lay scattered around the door. Lying there broken and abandoned, the pieces of wood felt more ominous than even Miss Hiss's angry words.

But nothing that Miss Hiss said, or could have said, compared to the look Sasha gave Vivian.

"What did Amanda say?" Sasha asked slowly. "That there were paints . . . stolen?"

She asked it as a question, but Vivian could tell she had an inkling about what the answer was already.

"Just let me explain," Vivian said quietly. "But let's go back to the cabin. There are too many people around."

"Explain what?" Sasha asked. "What happened, Vivian? Why is Amanda saying that about the paints? Did you . . . did you know?"

Vivian glanced around them, hoping the kids nearby couldn't hear the conversation. But most of them were too engrossed in Miss Hiss's temper tantrum to pay attention.

"Look, just, it's complicated. I didn't mean—it wasn't like that—if you just come back to the cabin and talk to me, I'll explain everything."

The expression on Sasha's face as the truth dawned was almost too much for Vivian to bear. And then Sasha snorted, and she didn't even sound like Sasha at all. She sounded older, and meaner, like the other girls in their cabin who rolled their eyes at her normal enthusiasm.

"I think I've maybe had enough of your 'explanations,' Vivian," she said in a very cold voice. "I think maybe I've had enough of you, too. Am I some kind of idiot? Is that what you think? Because I think you were the one who stole those paints. You were the one who took them from Amanda. And then you sold them to me and tried to take all my money. And now Amanda is gone, and the keys to the arts and crafts cabin are lost in the woods, and the only thing I liked about this stupid camp is probably ruined for the rest of the summer. And it's all your fault."

Vivian opened her mouth to reply. But she didn't have time to say anything, because Sasha had already stalked off.

ARCHIE

The whole camp was in disarray, and not just because of the caution tape and destroyed dock. Everyone was up, and yet there was no breakfast prepared, and no activities to do, and so the kids just milled around, or gathered in small clusters talking quietly. The counselors were huddled together by the main hall, having some kind of heated argument that Archie tried to eavesdrop on but couldn't make out.

And Miss Hiss stayed in her office.

"Why don't we go play cards or something?" Oliver asked. "Just to get away from all of . . . this." He waved his hand at the clumps of awkward campers and the messed-up dock.

Archie didn't answer, just stared listlessly into the woods, not seeing them. He wondered where Mitchell had gone.

As much as Archie wanted to blame him for the problems—Why had he talked about it with his cabinmates? And why had they believed him, and gone looking for the treasure?—his heart wasn't in it. He knew, deep down, why all of this had happened.

Because of him.

It was only supposed to be a con. A bet. A way to get one over on Vivian. It wasn't supposed to ruin the camp for everyone. But now there was no way they could use the lake for swimming and canoeing, and the woods were still closed off because of the bees, and if Amanda had really thrown away the only set of keys to the arts and crafts cabin then those activities were probably canceled too. The only things worth doing at Camp Shady Brook, all ruined.

As much as he pretended otherwise, Archie loved this place. And now . . . he couldn't bear to see the faces of the dejected campers who stood around aimlessly. If they didn't know it was all his fault, they would soon enough.

He was suddenly glad he couldn't find Mitchell. Mitchell was a nice kid, the opposite of a trouble-maker, and it was because of Archie that he'd gotten pulled into this. He wondered when Mitchell would figure out it was all a lie. Or maybe he had already.

Oliver snapped his fingers right in front of

Archie's eyes, startling him. "Oh good, so you're not in a coma," Oliver said. "I was beginning to wonder."

"Sorry," Archie said. "I'm just a little distracted."

"A little?" Oliver said with a laugh. "I get it, all of this is nuts, but there's nothing we can do right now, Arch. So why don't we take a walk, or go play a game, or do anything else other than standing around here staring off into space?"

"I don't feel like playing cards," Archie said. This was a little bit of a lie. He loved playing cards, mainly because his dad had taught him about a million different games, and most important, how to win at all of them.

"Then we'll do something else," Oliver said with more patience than usual. "But we're here to have fun, right? So let's have some, at least while we can. Even if it's not doing cons. Because I thought that having fun was the whole point, wasn't it? To have a good time? At least, that's the thing that mattered the most to me."

Archie considered this, looking at Oliver curiously. He'd always thought of Oliver as a sidekick, someone who hung out with him because of the scams and the money. Even when they talked on the phone during the school year it was always about the cons they'd pulled, or would pull, or stuff Archie had found out on the Internet about new scam techniques. But maybe, just maybe, Oliver wasn't just hanging out with him to get money out of gullible campers. Maybe he was just being a friend.

"It was fun," he admitted. But to Oliver's expectant look, Archie just shook his head. "Thanks," he said, and he meant it. "But maybe later."

"Suit yourself," Oliver said, and walked off toward the CIT cabins on the other side of the parking lot.

As Archie stood and watched him go, Vivian appeared at his elbow. "Come on," she hissed.

"Where?" he asked.

"The woods," she said. "We need to talk."

"The woods are closed off," Archie said.

Vivian made a face at him. "Now? Really? You're all of a sudden Mr. Rule Book?"

He had no answer to that, and so he just followed her back toward the woods, where they ducked under the caution tape but still kept a hefty distance from the old boathouse. He could hear a faint buzzing over the breeze and tried not to wince. The hurt from his bee stings was fading, but the memory was fresh enough in his mind.

Once they were safely away from the rest of the campers, Vivian said, "First, I want you to know that I won the bet."

Well, that was unexpected.

"You did?"

"Yeah," she said, but she didn't look happy. Actually, she looked miserable. "I got the money last night. But I don't care anymore. I'm giving it back."

"Okay . . ."

"Because the cons are over. The bet is over, and now we—"

"—have to fix this," he finished for her. It was the thought that had been forming in his head since he first looked at the broken dock this morning. He knew she was right. They'd gone too far. Both of them. "But how?"

Vivian pursed her lips. "I don't know. You're the idea person; you need to come up with something."

"But how do we fix a whole camp? We can't, like, hire a contractor. We're kids."

"I know," she said. "But we have to. You know we do."

His mind worked furiously. There had to be a way to get Miss Hiss to fix the camp herself—to put everything back to normal. There just had to.

And that's when he had his big idea. Maybe the best idea he'd ever had. A con to top all cons. Because it wasn't about him, it was about all the kids who had suffered enough for one summer—partly at his hands, he had to admit, but also thanks to Miss Hiss. Maybe there was a way to set everything right once and for all—and get back at the camp director, too. He remembered all those awards in her office.

Camp Director of the Year. He was pretty sure Miss Hiss would do literally anything, even fix broken-down Camp Shady Crook, to be honored like that again. And Archie knew just what he needed to do.

But to put his plan into action, he needed help.

And the best person to help was standing right in front of him.

"Are you ready for one more big scam?" he asked Vivian.

"I don't want to do scams anymore," she said. "I thought I made that clear."

"But this will be different," he said, thinking about what Oliver had said. "I'm beginning to think maybe it's time we start using our powers . . . for good."

VIVIAN

Once Archie had sketched out his plan to fix Camp Shady Crook, Vivian knew two things. First, this was the best idea he'd ever had. And second, she needed to find Sasha and explain.

Even though her stomach hurt at the very thought of confessing everything she'd done.

I have to do this, she kept telling herself. *I have to.*

The weirdest part was that hanging out with Archie, talking about what they were going to do next, as if they were a team instead of rivals, had been both extremely strange and yet also the most normal thing in the world. But she'd think about what that meant later. It was time to make things right with Sasha.

Sasha was sitting by herself on the step in front of the arts and crafts cabin. Vivian suspected she'd been trying the door to make sure it was really locked. Typical Sasha, looking for a silver lining.

But once she saw Vivian, her face told a different story.

"What do *you* want." It was a very blunt statement for Sasha. Vivian felt tears coming to her eyes when she heard the anger in Sasha's voice.

"Please." In her heart, Vivian willed her friend to stay put and not walk off. Just long enough for her to make things okay. "Please let me explain."

Sasha's face changed. "I guess that would be all right?" she said, sounding like the old Sasha, if only for a brief minute. "I mean, I'm still mad at you, but I do want to know . . . why. Why you did what you did."

And so, after taking a deep breath, Vivian told her everything. About Archie and the cons. About the fake chocolate bar, and the weird clothes. And Field Day, and getting the candy from Lily. And about the bet. About scamming Sasha. And about her plans to give the paints back once she won.

Sasha listened to most of the story silently. Vivian couldn't tell if she understood, or if she was mad, or really anything. It was excruciating to talk to someone like Sasha, who always had a smile or a comment, and get nothing back in return, except for a stony frown and silence.

Finally, Sasha spoke.

"A bet?" she asked. And she sounded way more

rueful and cynical than she'd ever sounded before, at least to Vivian. "So I was just, like, a chess piece in your little game with Archie? I can just picture you guys laughing about poor stupid Sasha, taking the bait. Great. How is that supposed to make me feel better?"

"That's not what I was doing! I was trying to stop Archie from conning the other kids."

"By conning me."

Her words hung in the air.

"I thought we were friends," Sasha said. Vivian realized that for the first time since they'd met, Sasha was talking in that flat, mean tone, the way girls like Lily talked. The way girls liked Margot talked. And in Sasha's words, she heard the echo of herself on the day she found out Margot was using her. The part of her that just shut down because anything else would mean crying, and she didn't want to cry, not in front of someone she thought was her friend, not in front of someone who had just made it perfectly plain that wasn't true.

Vivian shut her eyes. She didn't realize how much Sasha meant to her until this moment, and she was shocked by the prickly feeling of tears forming behind her eyelids. "I'm so sorry. And I do like you. I'm just really, really terrible at showing it."

Sasha said nothing. Vivian took another deep breath. It was now or never.

"Here's the thing," Vivian said. "I got in a lot of trouble last year at school, and that changed everything for me." She grabbed another gulp of air. "My friend Margot—well, I thought she was my friend—convinced me to help her break into the school and change her grades on the school computer."

Sasha gasped theatrically. Even with everything going on, she was still Sasha-from-the-Bus, after all. "You broke into your *school*?"

"Yeah," Vivian said. "And we got caught, naturally. I mean, I knew we would, I just never said it. I never stood up to Margot. And then, well, she blamed me for everything."

Vivian sank down a little into herself. "I was never good at making friends until I met Margot. It's just never been something I could do. I mean, sometimes people like being around me, but they don't want to be friends with me, not once they get to know me. But Margot and I both started our new middle school at the same time. She was like me—or at least I thought so. We had fun together, just goofing around. It was different than the kids in elementary school."

Sasha nodded. She still looked mad, but she didn't interrupt.

"But then it got weird. Margot always wanted to do stuff—trick people. Make trouble. At first it was fun. I'd never had a friend like that," she said, looking out at the woods but not really seeing them. "But when she got this idea we could change her grades—her parents were always on her case to do better in school—well, things went downhill fast." Vivian looked up. "I didn't do any of it, just so you know. I was just the lookout. I was just . . . Oliver, pretty much."

She paused. "But we got caught. Both of us. She was expelled and I was suspended, and then . . ." She trailed off again. "She told me she wasn't really my friend at all. She told me that I was annoying, and stupid, and that I'd messed everything up and she'd never really liked me. And you know, when she actually said it, it made sense. I knew she was right. She never seemed really interested in me, or what I liked, or what I wanted to do. It was always about her, and her ideas. And they were fun—until they weren't."

"And all this stuff with Archie and Oliver?" Sasha ventured.

"Was also fun." Vivian grimaced. "Until it wasn't. But the thing is—the most important thing—is now I know I have to fix it. Archie and I both do."

"Okay, that whole thing at your school, that sounds really hard? I feel bad about that, I do!" Sasha said. But then she made a little grumbling sound and said, "But how are you going to fix this? It's impossible!" She waved her hand around. From where they were sitting they could see the path down to Lake Joyless, usually thronged with kids heading toward the dock. But today it was empty and desolate, pieces of the dock still floating in the water. "Look at this place!"

"We've got a plan."

"Oh, you and Archie Drake? Count me out."

"It's a great plan!"

"Any plan that comes from you and Archie is, by definition, kind of a terrible plan? I mean, I'm just saying?"

"But this one is different!" Vivian didn't want to sound like she was pleading, but she was. The whole idea wouldn't be the same if Sasha still hated her. "And we need your help."

"My help? Me?" Sasha said. "I don't want to get in trouble! I think there's been enough trouble around here!"

"I won't let you get in trouble, I promise," Vivian said. "If we get caught, I'll make sure I'm the only one who gets any blame." She knew, from her days with Margot, how easy it was to be the one who gets blamed for everything.

"Okay, fine. I'll help you," Sasha said, more firmly than Vivian had heard her speak before. "I need to know what exactly you want me to do first, though! Because I don't really trust you."

"Understood."

Sasha gave a sad little laugh. "We could have had so much fun this summer, without all of this. I would have been your friend, you know."

And the thing was, Vivian did know. Which was maybe the hardest part.

ARCHIE

The next morning, after breakfast, Archie and Vivian called the first meeting of what he had named in his head: "Operation Fix Camp Shady Crook."

They met in the woods behind the caution tape again. At this point, a few bees were the least of their troubles. Even Archie could admit that.

Oliver came, of course, though he was skeptical that anything could be changed. "This is Miss Hiss we're talking about, right? The same Miss Hiss who declared hard taco shells were a safety hazard because they cost more money than she wanted to pay? The same Miss Hiss who makes eight-year-olds do push-ups if they talk out of turn in morning meeting? You've got to admit, this is not the same as getting some kid to give you peanut butter cups from their care package!"

He made one final plea to give up while they were waiting for the others to arrive. "It's over, Arch. It was fun while it lasted, but you have to accept that it's over now, and we need to figure out another way to have fun. Or is that just impossible for you?"

"I know it's over," Archie said quietly. "I know. But we just have to do one more big job. The one that will fix everything."

"Or get us all escorted off the premises and onto the next bus out of Vermont," Oliver said with a thin, worried smile.

Vivian insisted on bringing her friend Sasha, who, it appeared, now knew far more about what Archie had been up to than he was personally comfortable with. He privately wished he'd told her not to spread things around. Still, if he wanted Vivian's help, it was clear that Sasha was part of the package deal. And he definitely needed Vivian's help.

Besides, also joining the group was . . . Mitchell.

Archie had been surprised when Mitchell approached him at breakfast. Around him the kids were picking at cold cereal and trying to peel wrinkly and desiccated clementines, since nobody had cooked anything, and it didn't seem like anyone was going to make a proper meal for them anytime soon.

Archie had steeled himself for Mitchell's anger,

but instead the boy was filled with cold efficiency. "I know you lied to me. I know you tried to trick me," Mitchell said matter-of-factly. "And we'll talk about that later. But right now I'm more worried about the trouble you've caused. That we've caused. So, tell me, how are you going to fix this?"

Archie took a deep breath. He wasn't sure Mitchell could really understand all of what Archie had been up to, but he was becoming convinced they needed as many kids they could trust to make their plan work. And the plan had to work—he was sure of that now. So he told Mitchell to come to their meeting.

"What are you doing here?" Mitchell asked when he saw Oliver. Archie forgot for a moment that kids like Mitchell had no idea of the depths his machinations. Part of him was secretly pleased by that. But for this con, it just meant more explanations.

"It's a long story," Oliver said with a grunt. "But I'm here to help."

"And we're going to need a lot of help," Vivian said, cutting off the question Mitchell was poised to ask. "Archie has a plan and it's a good one, but to make it happen we'll need to do two things—and for the first one, we need some pictures of the camp to send to the Beaumonts. The people who own the place. The people who hired Miss Hiss. The only people who can take her down, for good."

"But how can we take pictures?" Sasha asked. "Nobody has a camera. They were all confiscated the first day of camp."

"Ah, but that's where you're mistaken," Vivian said with a smile, and she pulled out the small digital camera she'd kept hidden in her bunk since the beginning of the summer. "I've already filled this with pictures of everything—the dock, the weeds in the lake, the horrible mess hall. Even the caution tape around the woods."

Sasha looked at her with admiration, but then Mitchell spoke up.

"Okay, I get there's a plan. I get that you guys want to fix things, and that's cool. The thing I don't get," Mitchell said, "is why any of this happened in the first place. I mean, I thought you were rich—the famous Archie Drake." He sounded genuinely perplexed.

Archie let out a long breath. He'd woven so many stories it was almost impossible now to do anything except tell the truth. Even to Mitchell the Unconnable.

"I'm not," he said. "Well, I am Archie Drake, that's my name. But I'm not famous. Or rich. Or related to anyone who is famous or rich. Honestly, I don't even know anyone who is famous or rich. I met one of the Mets once, but it was for, like, two seconds. The reality is, I'm just a regular kid. From Trenton, New

Jersey. And I've been fooling people here for years."

"What?" Mitchell's face was truly astonished. "But I thought—you said—everybody said—"

"Everybody's wrong." Archie couldn't help but think about Alicia and the twins, and how he'd tried to hide them when they visited for Parents' Day. The memory made him wince. It wasn't just that he'd tried to pretend to be someone else; it was that he'd denied who he really was—even to the point of acting like his own family didn't exist. He was starting to understand that now. He wasn't the fake person he pretended to be at camp. He was the same person here, and everywhere, however much he tried to fight it. But he was still Archie Drake. And that had to count for something.

"But why?" Mitchell asked. "Why did you pretend to be someone else?"

That was the big question. Why? Why had he pretended he was someone other than himself for so long, and to so many people? It was impossible to explain—the envy, the anger, the stupid grudges he'd held against everyone he'd ever met who he thought was better than he was. He had no answer.

But Vivian did.

"Basically, Archie's a con artist," she said. "But I think he might be reforming. I hope he is. Anyway, just work with it, for now. We have a job to do."

Her words jolted Archie back to the meeting and the task at hand.

"And now it's time for one last big con," Archie said. "The best yet."

Vivian and Archie high-fived.

The rest of the kids looked unimpressed. Including Oliver.

"So, I get that we want to show the Beaumonts what's really going on here," Oliver said. "But Archie said we're also going to try to convince Miss Hiss she's won a contest—the best camp director of the year, or something like that. Why don't we just send the pictures Vivian took to the Beaumonts? Why go through all the trouble of making her think she's won something? I'd rather not make her happy, even for one minute."

"Because we want her to fix everything," Vivian said with exaggerated patience. "And fix it right away—the bees, the dock, the arts and crafts cabin. If we wait until the Beaumonts show up we have no idea what's going to happen or when. And then the whole summer will be ruined—not just for us, but for all the other campers. For everyone. And isn't that the whole point? Not just to get Miss Hiss in trouble, but to make everything better again. And if she's convinced she's won an award—and that people are coming to give it to her, and maybe that there'll be newspapers and stuff who want to write about the camp—then she'll definitely do everything she can to fix this mess. How could she not? Nobody's going to give an award to a camp that looks like this, no matter how many excuses Miss Hiss gives. So she'll fix everything, as soon as she can. I'm sure of it."

Archie gave the group a grim smile. Truth was, the looks on the faces of his fellow campers when they realized the dock was destroyed had been haunting him. Even the kids who did it hadn't really thought they'd break the whole thing—just remove a piece or two. All because of his stupid story about treasure. All because of his stupid bet with Vivian. All because he'd thought that getting a few dollars or some candy bars was more important than what anyone else wanted.

And now Vivian, Oliver, Sasha, and Mitchell were all looking at him like he was a leader. Not because they thought he was rich or important, or because he told them a compelling lie, the way most kids looked at him. But because he had a plan.

It was hard to believe that just a few weeks ago he would have been mostly on his own, with only occasional company from Oliver. Now he had a whole group of people helping him with his latest scam—and it wasn't even a scam, really, more like retribution for the entire camp.

Maybe even retribution for him.

He took a deep breath. There was no time for regrets now, he had a job to do.

"Of course, it all has to look totally legit," he said. "The letter from the Camp Association, the envelope, everything. Miss Hiss will notice all the details. We don't want there to be any chance she'll see through the plan until the final moment. And remember, she's already suspicious about what's been going on this summer—and of me. So nothing can go wrong."

"I'm not good at lying, but I'm good at drawing!" Sasha said. "Could you get me one of those long envelopes? You know, the official kind?"

"Business envelope," Archie interjected. Sasha rolled her eyes at him in a very un-Sasha-like way.

"Business envelope, right!" she said. "And I'll make it look completely official—a postmark, maybe even a logo on the back?"

"But we also have to get these pictures to the Beaumonts," Vivian said, holding up her contraband camera. "Do you think you could download them on Miss Hiss's computer and e-mail them or something? Then they could see them right away."

Oliver shook his head vigorously. "No e-mail," he said. "All the e-mails that are addressed to the Beaumonts go straight to Miss Hiss; she set it up that way so nobody could complain about her, and so she could handle anyone who tried."

"But there has to be some way to reach them," Vivian said. "They live in Boston, right?"

Archie nodded slowly. "I'm sure if anyone has their address, it's Miss Hiss. We could print them out and send them with a note."

"But doesn't Miss Hiss go through all the mail before it gets picked up?" Mitchell asked. "She'll definitely notice if we're sending a letter to her boss. I mean, she's evil, but she's not stupid."

Archie frowned. "You have a point," he said. "We'll need to have someone go into town and mail it from there."

"Go into town?" Vivian said. "That's impossible."

The kids stared dejectedly at one another. Sending the pictures to the Beaumonts was key to getting back at Miss Hiss. Sure, they wanted her to fix the camp. But they also wanted to take her down, for good. And even Archie was at a loss. There was no way he was going to get any of the counselors to take him into town, not after everything that had happened this summer. And Vivian was in just as much trouble, if not more.

VIVIAN

Maybe I could go," Mitchell said slowly.

"You?" Archie asked.

"Yeah," he said, with more confidence this time. "I'd get Nick the Nurse to take me. I'll tell him I need a refill for my asthma inhaler; my mom sent the prescription to the pharmacy in town just in case I needed more. She told me before I came."

Oliver looked a little skeptical. "Nick is just going to say he can get it for you. He won't take you with him all the way into town."

But now Sasha spoke, and with such surety that Vivian looked at her with awe. "Mitchell can just say they need to make sure to get the right kind, that sometimes people mess it up—or he needs to ask the pharmacist a question about the dosages," she said. "Trust me—I know all about allergies. Nick will do whatever it takes to make sure Mitchell has his meds."

Vivian didn't know what to say. If she'd learned anything in the past two days it was she she'd clearly underestimated Sasha. And Archie, for that matter. She looked around at the little group—they were all smiling and nodding at Sasha's little plan. Had she also misjudged Oliver? And Mitchell?

For most of the summer Vivian had assumed that the other kids had no interest in being her friend, so there was no point in trying. But maybe the reason why she didn't get along with the other kids wasn't because they disliked her . . . but because she acted like she didn't like them. It was an uncomfortable thought. But Vivian had been having a lot of uncomfortable thoughts lately.

Maybe that was the whole reason why she didn't have anyone at school except Margot. Maybe it wasn't because she was a terrible person, but because she wasn't open to the people around her. People like Sasha.

"So I'll get into the office tonight," Archie said. "And get the Beaumonts' address and print out all the pictures. Vivian and Sasha will need to get the letter together after lights out. Could you be ready to go tomorrow, Mitchell?"

Mitchell took a deep breath, and nodded.

"But why does he get to do everything?" Oliver

asked. "I mean, this is serious stuff. If we mess this up, the whole plan is ruined."

Mitchell and Sasha exchanged a look, one Vivian couldn't decipher. Then Sasha spoke. "You guys are great at cons, there's no contest there," she said. "But maybe now's different. Maybe now, for something like this you need people with different skills—people like me and Mitchell?"

Archie spoke up, and his voice sounded different somehow. Almost . . . nice.

"You may have a point," he said. "Maybe it's time for us to accept that you guys are the only ones who can really make this work."

ARCHIE

The next day the first steps of their plan were put into action. The final con at Camp Shady Crook. And if everything worked out the way Archie had devised, the best one yet.

Because for once, it wasn't about him hurting his fellow campers. It was about helping them.

The counselors had finally managed to pull together a few activities for the campers, despite the limited resources with half the camp, including the lake, unusable. They set up some board games in the main hall, and organized tag and other outdoor activities in the parking lot. Tina, the counselor for the Brook Trouts, had found some pens and scrap paper so some of the kids could draw, even though the arts and crafts cabin remained locked up tight.

Miss Hiss had been holed up either in her office

or her house since her outburst the day before. But every single person at Camp Shady Brook knew it was only a matter of time before she had more to say, and that, along with the destruction that surrounded them, formed a layer of gloom over all the proceedings. Even the little kids were quiet and subdued as they scratched with sticks in the dirt.

But with some help from Oliver, Vivian and Archie had managed to get the letter about the "Best Camp Director in Vermont" contest put in with Miss Hiss's regular mail.

They'd all admired Sasha's handiwork just that morning. Thanks to the letter Vivian had written, typed up and printed by Archie in his midnight trip to the office, and Sasha's beautiful artwork—she even creased the envelope so it looked like it had gone through the mail—there was no way that Miss Hiss could suspect the letter was anything but legitimate. Or so they hoped. They all watched eagerly that morning as the camp director sorted through the pile of mail she had brought to her table at breakfast. Archie swore he saw a glimmer of a smile on her stony face as she opened one of the envelopes, but he couldn't be sure—and he didn't want to get caught staring.

Mitchell had stepped in afterward, and after a whispered conference with Nick at breakfast, had managed to cadge a ride into town, the package of printed-out pictures and a note to the Beaumonts safely stowed in his pocket.

So all that was left to do was wait.

Archie was at loose ends. He was usually confident when he was in the middle of a con, his mind working over all the possibilities. But this con felt different. And not only different. Important.

What if they failed? What if Miss Hiss saw through their plan to convince her to fix the camp for this made-up award ceremony, or what if the Beaumonts didn't care about the pictures, or what if a million other things went wrong? Camp Shady Brook would be ruined forever and it would be all his fault. Even if most of the kids didn't know that, he knew it. The thought haunted him.

"Wanna go see if the Bluegills are going to play Ultimate Frisbee today?" Mitchell asked him after lunch. "I bet they'd let you play too."

Archie sighed, deep and long. "Could you just stop?"

"Stop what?"

"Stop being nice to me."

Mitchell looked alarmed. "Why . . . ? What's wrong with being nice to you?"

Archie groaned. "Because I don't deserve it. All I've ever done is try to scam you. I'm a horrible person. Having you be all nice to me is not making that any better!"

"You're not a horrible person, Archie."

"Are you for real?" Archie asked.

"Because I'm being nice to you?" Mitchell laughed. "You really are something, you know. Can't people just be nice? Without having some sort of secret agenda?"

Archie didn't know how to answer that. He'd always thought nice people were, in a word, delusional. He never really thought that sometimes people were just nice because it was a good way to be.

But his thoughts were interrupted when he saw a couple of workers he'd never seen before carrying two-by-fours and boxes of tools. They marched past the kids with a self-important air, like people with a job to do. All the way down the path to the broken dock.

"It worked," Archie breathed.

"What?" Mitchell asked.

"It worked. The plan. It worked."

VIVIAN

That afternoon Vivian sat with Sasha, casually watching some of the Longnose Gars listlessly bounce a rubber ball around in the dusty parking lot.

"I guess what I still don't understand is why you just couldn't have fun?" Sasha asked, suddenly. "Fun doing normal things, like swimming and crafts and roasting marshmallows! Fun like everybody else! Instead of trying to beat everyone at some game that nobody else wanted to play?"

Vivian frowned. "Maybe I'm still trying to figure out the answer to that myself."

Despite her regrets about the summer, talking to Sasha was more like talking to a real friend than Vivian had done in a long time. She felt like she'd had some sort of mask over her eyes, and now it was finally gone, and she could see everything more clearly. Even if what she saw was all the mistakes she'd made.

And as she looked out over the parking lot, a strange truck pulled up the long drive and parked right in front of the main building.

The little kids stopped bouncing their ball and everyone gathered around to gawk. PHIPPS CONTRACTING, the truck said on the side. Two men got out of the truck and, without seeming to notice the kids, headed straight for the main office.

"What do you think that's all about?" Sasha asked.

Vivian tried not to get her hopes up, but she had a glimmer of an idea of what was going on. "Not completely sure," she said. "But it might just mean Miss Hiss got her letter."

The next week was a haze of activity around the camp.

Workers were everywhere—ripping up the roots to lay a new path down to the lake, where other workers were building a new dock. Two women covered in spacesuits made out of netting were setting up barriers near the old boathouse. "Stay back," one of them barked. "We're removing some hives."

Vivian marveled at how quickly Miss Hiss was able to get people to come out and fix things, once she put her mind to it. "Amazing, if you think about it."

"She probably threw them a ton of money," Archie said. "With all the cash families pay to send their kids here, she's got to have piles of it. I guess she just never saw any point in using it before. At least not for the camp."

The two of them were headed toward the old playing field behind the lake to play Frisbee. New sod had been laid across it in neat rows, like carpet. The past few days of hanging out with him was almost like she and Archie had been friends since the beginning of the summer, instead of sworn enemies since barely a week ago.

A cleaning crew tackled the cobwebs and dirty corners of the mess hall. Landscapers picked up the trash and weeds and put sweet-smelling mulch on the paths to cover up the rocks.

Even the cabins got a once-over. The Rainbow Smelts got a new mirror to replace the cracked one, bright lavender shower curtains, new window screens, and a brand-new screen door. A young woman with a drill came in after breakfast and replaced all the bolts in the various bunk beds so they no longer tipped and shook like the cabin was on a ship at sea.

"What's this all about?" Patrice, Lily's friend, kept asking. But Lily looked as confused as she was. "Why are they suddenly fixing everything?"

"I guess Miss Hiss wanted to make the place nice

again?" Sasha said with an enigmatic smile. "It's about time, don't you think?"

That Saturday, before the buses came to take some of the campers away, Miss Hiss made a special announcement.

The mess hall had been transformed. All the cobwebs were gone, and the entire place was scrubbed clean. The tables had been reorganized to allow kids to walk freely between them, instead of all clustered together, and each table had cute metal pails of silverware and condiments, labeled in chalk with swirling letters.

"It actually worked," Vivian murmured to the girl next to her. "It actually worked."

"What worked?" the girl said.

"Never mind," Vivian replied.

Outside the mess hall many of them had noticed a truck with a picture of a cornucopia of vegetables and fruits on the side. MARIGOLD CATERING, it said in shiny letters. Workers were busy pulling out trays and bins. And whatever they were making for breakfast smelled better than anything they had ever had at Camp Shady Brook before.

"Good morning, campers," Miss Hiss said as she strode to the front of the room, and she looked completely different. Almost . . . happy.

Which didn't mean she wasn't still terrifying.

Just terrifying in a different way.

"As you may have noticed, we've had a lot of activity here at Camp Shady Brook over the past few days," Miss Hiss announced. "I want you all to know that I'm pleased to say that all of our facilities will be up and running later today."

The kids looked at their plates. A few hardy, or extremely hungry, souls used the opportunity to grab surreptitious forkfuls of the strawberry pancakes and cheesy eggs, before looking back up at Miss Hiss, who seemed like she expected them to do something. A few began to dutifully clap.

The camp director smiled as though she'd received a standing ovation.

"I'm also very honored to be able to tell you that I, your camp director"—here she gave a very large self-satisfied smile—"have been chosen as the recipient of the Best Camp Director Award by the Summer Camp Association of America! It's an extremely high honor, and the award ceremony will be here, at the camp, tomorrow afternoon. There will be some local newspapers coming to cover it, of course, so I want to make sure we put our best foot forward, as a camp." She gave a searching look around. "That means you're all going to be on our very best behavior, and dressed in your nicest Camp Shady Brook T-shirts. If you don't have one, then we can . . . arrange something with the camp store."

Even in her joy at her upcoming prize, Miss Hiss looked pained at the idea of giving out more free T-shirts. But clearly, the sacrifice was worth it.

As Archie passed Vivian's table on the way to the food line for seconds, he gave her a bright, satisfied smile. But all he said was, "Hook, line, and sinker."

ARCHIE

As the kids dug into their breakfast, very few people noticed the door to the mess hall open and an elderly couple slowly walk in and make their way to the front of the room where Miss Hiss was still talking.

Even Miss Hiss didn't seem to notice the strangers at first. "And I don't want you talking to anyone without my permission, but a few lucky campers will get to be interviewed about our wonderful camp. As long as I can trust you," she added, with a glare that felt more comfortable to most of them than the smile she'd been wearing through much of her speech.

The older lady who had just walked in the door cleared her throat. "Hello, Philomena."

Miss Hiss snapped to attention. "Joyce!" she said, rushing toward the couple to clasp their hands. "Harold! What a nice surprise! Everyone, this is Mr. and Mrs. Beaumont, the owners and founders of our own beloved Camp Shady Brook!"

She turned back to the couple. "Are you here for the awards ceremony? It's not until tomorrow, I'm afraid. We're just getting ready."

"What ceremony?" the man asked.

"The Camp Director Award—I assume you got a letter as well," Miss Hiss said.

"Oh yes," Mrs. Beaumont said. "We got a letter all right."

Miss Hiss gave a broad, fake smile, more like a crocodile than a person. "So you know all about it." She glanced around at the children. "See how excited everyone is? We've been having a wonderful summer. So glad you are here to enjoy it."

"Have you?" Mrs. Beaumont asked. She also smiled at the children, but when her face turned to Miss Hiss, it was a mask of anger.

Miss Hiss fell silent.

Then Mr. Beaumont walked forward. He was very old and slow, but he had a certain stiffness to his back that made everyone in the room sit up a little straighter.

"We're not here about an award, Philomena," he said. "We're here about . . . this."

He pulled some papers out of his jacket pocket and unfolded them carefully.

Archie was pretty sure he knew what they were. From across the room, Mitchell caught his eye, and smiled.

"Bees in the boathouse? Children unable to swim in the lake? Half the camp unusable? And nothing but scraps and leftovers for dinner?" Mr. Beaumont thrust the papers at Miss Hiss. "This is not what Camp Shady Brook is about. This is not what we hired you for."

Miss Hiss began looking through the photos on the pages, first slowly, then frantically. "Where did these come from? There are no cameras allowed at Camp Shady Brook."

"We can see why now," Mrs. Beaumont said dryly. "I think it's time we had a little . . . chat . . . about how you've been running things while we've been gone."

"A private chat," Mr. Beaumont added. He touched Miss Hiss's arm and she recoiled. "In particular, I'd like to go more closely over the camp accounts, Philomena. We've trusted you for far too long. All those times you've said we couldn't afford to keep our scholarship students because of all the improvements you had to make—well, we understandably have a lot of questions. Many, many questions."

"I don't know what you're talking about—this is slander and lies—the children are having a wonderful breakfast, the camp looks great—"She gave a strong glare around the room at all the campers. "If anyone here has anything to say about how the summer is going, I'm sure they'd be happy to speak up.

"In fact," she continued, her voice getting stronger, "I think if you ask any camper in this room they will tell you this camp is the best place they've ever been. Look around! It's beautiful. Those photos are doctored, they're a fraud. Someone here is playing a trick—a cruel trick. Everyone here knows that." She glared again at the campers.

The kids shifted in their seats. Many of them looked at the ground. Nobody wanted to stand up to Miss Hiss, even now, with the Beaumonts there. They were too afraid of what she might do.

Except Mitchell. Mitchell the Unconnable O'Connor.

Archie held his breath and watched as Mitchell stood up from his table, even as the rest of the kids looked like they wanted to sink into the floor.

"Sorry to interrupt, but I have to speak up," Mitchell said.

"You do not have permission to speak," Miss Hiss said sharply.

"You just said we could speak. And I'm not trying to speak to you," Mitchell said in a very brave voice. "I want to speak to . . . them."

He walked to the front of the room, and took a deep breath. "She's lying," he said to the Beaumonts, but loud enough that every single kid in the room heard.

"What?" Miss Hiss said. "What are you talking about? This is impossible. Sit down right now!"

But Mitchell only stood up straighter. Out of the corner of his eye, Archie saw Vivian cover her mouth in surprise. But Archie was less surprised. Somehow, he always knew Mitchell had it in him.

"This place has been a mess all summer and it's only gotten worse," Mitchell told the Beaumonts. "Everything in those pictures is true. She only fixed it up because she thought she was winning an award and the newspaper was coming."

"He's lying, he's a liar, he's a terrible liar, that boy," Miss Hiss sputtered. "We all know it, he's always making up stories right and left. The absolute worst. He really should have been sent home weeks ago. I'll be contacting his parents directly, I assure you!"

"I'm not a liar," Mitchell said quietly.

"He's not," Archie said, getting up himself from the Walleyes table and walking over to stand behind Mitchell. "He's probably the most honest kid at this camp. I should know."

Miss Hiss whirled around. "You! And who's going to listen to you? You've been causing trouble since the first day! Taking money, and candy—going out of bounds. I'm sure the Beaumonts would be very interested in hearing what you've been up to." Her voice changed as she turned back to the Beaumonts. "I'm just too forgiving, that's the problem. The kids get in trouble and I can't bear to send them home. But that is going to change right now." She gave a long, slow look over the rest of the campers, as though daring them to contradict her.

Vivian and Sasha were sitting together at the Rainbow Smelts' table. After a quick series of glances back and forth, they both stood at the same time.

"He's telling the truth," Vivian said.

Sasha nodded her head emphatically. "Mitchell never lies! It's, like, his thing!"

"Sit down!" Miss Hiss snapped. "I order you all to sit down right now or you'll be sent to your cabins without breakfast!"

"Let them speak, Philomena," Mrs. Beaumont said.

It wasn't a request, it was an order.

Oliver stepped around from behind the food serving line and came to stand with Archie. He didn't say anything, but he stared at Miss Hiss with a forceful look.

Slowly, one by one at first, but then in larger groups, all of the other campers began to stand too. Within moments, the entire group was standing behind Mitchell, staring at the camp director wordlessly.

Mrs. Beaumont gave them all a big smile, then turned to Miss Hiss, her face changing to a grim frown.

"As I said, I think we should talk. Privately," she said to Miss Hiss.

"I'm sorry, children, for everything," Mr. Beaumont said to the room. "But we're going to fix it. For now, enjoy your breakfast."

"NO," Miss Hiss boomed. "I've run this camp for years. I just won an award. You can't march me out of here like a camper who has misbehaved."

"Last time I checked, we're the ones who own this place," Mr. Beaumont said calmly. "And we can do whatever we want."

He placed his hand gently on Miss Hiss's arm, and guided her out of the mess hall, Mrs. Beaumont at his side.

Before the door even closed behind them, the entire camp erupted in cheers.

VIVIAN

The last two weeks of camp were as much fun as the kids could have ever imagined, and they passed in a blur of happy activity. Miss Hiss was gone—they had no idea where, but most of them didn't care. But the lack of her angry face lifted everyone's spirits.

The Beaumonts moved into the house on the hill, but they were a constant presence around camp. Asking kids their names, cheering on the games, and always ready with a kind word. Mr. Beaumont was obviously very sick, but even he took time to talk to as many kids as possible.

Mrs. Beaumont got a locksmith to open up the arts and crafts cabin and let kids use all of the supplies they wanted. "Paints!" Sasha sighed happily. "And clay and fabric and cool colored pencils!"

Plus, right after Miss Hiss left, Mr. Beaumont went into town, and the next day there were three brand-new canoes, plus a kayak, and even better, a big bouncy float in the middle of the lake that kids could swim out to and then jump off from. There was a constant stream of kids bouncing and jumping all during the daylight hours.

And every single night there was a bonfire.

Swimming, canoeing, drawing, and painting. Almost like a whole summer packed into fourteen days. It was everything camp should be, and as the countdown to the last day of camp came closer, Vivian remembered how much she'd dreaded Camp Shady Brook, and how desperately she'd wanted to leave. But now it felt like the summer had flown by, and she couldn't imagine going home.

When Vivian did have free time, she'd mainly spent it hanging out with Sasha and Archie. Already they were planning on texting each other when they got home, and Vivian had invited them both to come visit her in New York. At meals the kids no longer sat with their bunkmates; instead they could mix it up as much as they wanted, so the girls sat with Archie and Mitchell and even Oliver sometimes—CITs didn't have to serve food anymore, since the Beaumonts decided to keep the catering service Miss Hiss had hired. "We'll get in a proper cook next year," Mrs. Beaumont told the kids. "But for now, this seems to be working out, right? You kids are liking the food?"

Most of them were too busy eating to do more than nod emphatically.

The last time Vivian saw Archie at Camp Shady Brook was when they were both getting on the buses to leave, for good. She gave him a wry smile, and came over to say good-bye.

"I guess this is it," she said to him as they waited for their turn to board the buses.

He smiled, and they both looked around at the busy campers, sharing addresses and promises to write, as the counselors darted back and forth with pieces of luggage, trying, and failing, to bring order to the mayhem that surrounded them. It was weird to finally be leaving.

It seemed like only yesterday Vivian was standing in this exact spot, plotting how to get all these kids to do stuff for her. And now it seemed like half of them were her friends. And the ones that weren't, well, she kind of wished they were.

"Any regrets?" Archie asked her.

"Tons," she said.

"Me too," he replied. "But in a way, it was the most fun I'd ever had."

She smiled at him. "You're insane, you know that?"

He didn't reply, but just looked out at the camp again.

"So, um," Archie said finally. "I guess this is good-bye."

He looked different standing there with his hands in his pockets. Almost like the awkward act he put on for marks, but also completely not like that at all.

"Yeah," Vivian said. She didn't quite know what to say to him. They'd been through a lot more than she'd ever imagined that first day, when he'd told her she had to follow the rules or else. The thought made her giggle.

Talk about first impressions gone wrong.

"Thanks for everything," he said. "I mean it. I don't know if I'm going to be coming back next year—I have a lot of things I need to explain to my dad, and especially my stepmom—but I'm still not sorry about the way things worked out."

"Me either," she said. She'd been entertaining the thought of asking her parents to send her back, especially now that the camp had changed so much, but the idea of Camp Shady Brook without Archie Drake seemed impossible to contemplate. Even if he was reformed.

"Anyway," Archie said slowly. "I have something for you."

"Really?" She gave him an incredulous look and wondered, for a second, if this wasn't one of his little tricks. But the look on his face was too genuine.

He pulled something out of his pocket and handed it to her. "It's not much. . . ."

She looked down. It was the multitool hair clip, the one she'd admired so much in the camp store the first time they ever went in there. The day he began to teach her how to be a con artist. It seemed like a lifetime ago.

She smiled, but then said slowly, "I don't know if I'll need this. I think my days of crime are behind me." She tried to hand it back, but he wouldn't take it, just kept his hands shoved in his pockets and kicked at the dirt.

"You don't have to use it for cons, you know," he said. "You can just use it for fun. To make things. Or fix things. To do things with friends."

The word hung there.

"Friends," she said.

"Friends," he replied.

She wondered if things would be different once she got back to New York. She knew it wasn't going to be easy, to go back to school and start over. But maybe everyone felt that way sometimes. Maybe even someone like Archie.

She looked at the clip again. "But I can't take it—I can't. It cost twenty dollars! That's got to be most of the money you made this summer."

"Yeah, especially since I think I'm going to give it all back."

"What?"

"It doesn't feel right anymore," he said, looking around at all the happy campers around them. She knew what he meant more than she could say.

But she still gave him a searching look. "Are you saying that your days of crime are finally behind you? No more Archie Drake, Man of a Thousand Scams?"

He shrugged. "Maybe I'm just tired of it all." He paused. "Maybe it's not all it's cracked up to be, taking things from people. Maybe there are better ways to have fun."

For once, even Vivian couldn't argue.

"Anyway, Oliver paid for it. I think he likes you!"

That's when she punched him in the arm.

Acknowledgments

One of the great joys of writing another book is getting a chance to thank all the wonderful people I've gotten to know since the last time I wrote my acknowledgments—and thank again the many people who have stuck with me through my writing career.

I especially appreciate the team at Aladdin, including editors Amy Cloud and Alyson Heller, art director Laura Lyn DiSiena, and artist Andy Smith, who all worked so hard to bring this book to life. I also want to thank my agent, Bridget Smith, whose notes on early drafts of this book helped me find the heart in the humor, and who always finds an answer to even my most pesky questions.

I've been lucky to get to know a lot of great authors in the past few years that have supported me as a friend and fellow writer, including Monica Tesler, Laura Shovan, Bridget Hodder, Jenn Bishop, Jennifer Maschari, Janet Johnson, Jen Malone, Jeff Zentner, MarcyKate Connolly, Victoria Coe, Elly Swartz, Erin Petti, and the rest of the Boston kidlit crew.

Someone in New York asked me, "Do all the children's book writers in Boston know each other?" — and it's true, we do!

Several friends read this manuscript in its early stages, including Brenda St John Brown, Jennifer Ray, and Greg Katsoulis. It was Greg's willingness to brainstorm about this book early on that helped me narrow down the concept and the original title—I'm still bummed we didn't end up using it.

A countless number of people have supported me as an author and a person but I especially need to highlight Minda Martin Zwerin, Crissy Adams, Deb Dwinell, Nicole Paul, Toya Williford, Laura Burrows, Marc Hachadourian, and Jenn Katsoulis, as well as my friends at Team Excel Synchronized Skating and the American Red Cross.

I also thank all the readers, of all ages, who read *The Last Boy at St. Edith's* and enjoyed it.

I'm particularly grateful to my parents, Don and Judy Gjertsen, my sister, Dina Gjertsen, and my in-laws, Eleanor and Dan Malone, for their constant encouragement.

And of course, lots of thanks and love to my husband Scott Malone and our daughter Nora for putting up with me through first drafts, revisions, copy edits, and more. It's no picnic living with a writer, but they make it look easy.

About the Author

Lee Gjertsen Malone is an author and journalist who has written about everything from why people hiccup to high-level finance. A non-native New Englander, she spent most of her early life in Long Island, Brooklyn, and Ithaca, New York. Lee likes traveling, animals, making cheese, volunteering, and overly complicated baking projects. She lives in Cambridge, Massachusetts, with her husband and daughter in a house where the people are outnumbered by the pets.